Serving Up INNOCENCE

Serving Up Innocence
Published by H.M. Shander

Cover Design: Casey Roop of Pink Ink Designs
Editing by: Infinite Phoenix Editing & IDIM Editorial
Shander, H.M., 1975—Serving Up Innocence

To my family
for always believing in me
and allowing me to
follow my dreams.

Table of Contents

Chapter One

The beat-up masonry with its chipped brick façade and windows caked in streaks of dirt from the longest, coldest winter on record indicated a dive; a hole in the ground, a joke of a place. But looks are deceiving. Always.

It was a blustery day in early March when I timidly walked into the main entrance of Westside, a restaurant many enjoyed as they were famous for their steak bowls. Even in the winter, people lined up for over an hour to wait for a table. Something I had done with my family on many occasions. However today I wouldn't be dining. I'd be starting my first shift as a waitress.

Money was tight and stretched thin. Tuition for my first semester of college hung in the air. With my current job, my daytime job, my hours had been cut back and that didn't help in the finance department. Bills were being paid because I didn't need creditors chasing me down, but I was only making the minimum monthly payments. I couldn't afford more than that and still live on my own. I hoped that by securing a waitressing job, the tips would help, and I could get a handle on things and not have to apply for a student loan. I hadn't worked my ass off only to falter now.

The warm air hit me in the face as I entered Westside, as did the tantalizing smells of grilled steak and spices. Suddenly I craved the taste of a Coririka Steak Supreme bowl. It wouldn't be in the cards today though. Instead, I tiptoed past the hostess podium searching for the boss but feeling as though I were breaking an unwritten rule.

"Can I help you?" A lady with a long, blondish braid asked in my direction. Her name tag stated Joy.

"I'm looking for Niall. Today's my first day." I swallowed down the penetrating crack in my voice. I wasn't a people person in the slightest, but I needed this job and stepping outside my comfort zone was what I'd have to do.

"He's in the back office." She pointed beyond the cash register, and past the cooking station to a place I couldn't see.

I took a step but hesitated. "Am I supposed to just go?"

"Yeah. Why not? You're one of us now, right?" A warm, infectious smile lingered on her face as her slender arm held a stack of laminated menus.

I tucked my confusion back into head and marched in the direction she pointed out, throwing my shoulders back and lifting my head. If I was going to act like I belonged there, I may as well have an air of confidence about me.

Unfamiliar eyes from the kitchen paid me no attention as I strutted over to the group. Putting my bravest face on, instead of the quivering mass I wanted to be, I spotted Niall, the manager who had interviewed me a week ago. I extended my hand as I reached him.

"Hello, Niall," I made sure I kept my voice from showing anything but fear.

The man beside Niall broke into a grin. "Shayne, right?"

"Yeah," I said, unable to form anything more coherent.

The man was gorgeous. Long dark dreads, a scruffy week-old beard that appeared well maintained and dark, brown eyes that dazzled in my direction. Standing slightly taller than me, he wore the standard issue Westside polo shirt in emerald green. It did nothing to hide the well-defined bulges in his upper arms and across his chest. This man was clearly a specimen to be worshipped, like a Greek God. And he had served my family last time I was here. He was flirty and fun and had singled me out as the mark of all his corny puns and winks.

I blinked several times to stop my eyes from drying out. It was terrible how I stared. If I was now going to work with the god, I'd better get used to seeing him and stop acting like such a crazy, hormone driven teenager. Okay, teenager was a bit of a stretch. I was nineteen, almost twenty. At the end of that tumultuous period of my life. My roaring twenties lay ahead of me, undefined and ready for all the adventures I planned on having. But first, bills needed to get paid. Which was why I snapped myself out of my headspace. He was now a co-worker and messing with coworkers was always trouble. My older brother Sean had told me as much, and he was wise. I learned from his mistake.

"I'm Jasper."

"Shayne," I said, reflexively as he shook my hand.

He chuckled. "Yeah, I know."

"Right." *I'm an idiot.* I looked over to Niall.

The manager was shorter than me, which wasn't saying much as I was pretty tall at 5'9", but still, I could see the start of a bald spot on his blond head. Stocky too, as his mid-section wasn't as defined as Jasper's.

Niall rifled through a box he'd retrieved off the shelf and tossed me the standard issue polo and a server's apron. "Both come to work every day clean. If size is a problem, grab the one that fits best, but you look like a medium." He pointed toward the bathroom. "Get changed first, and we'll get started."

When nothing more was said, I assumed he meant for me to change right now, so I disappeared into the staff bathroom a kitchen worker pointed out, and quickly pulled the green shirt on, which fit a little loose as I was no medium. That would imply I had a chest to fill it out, however the breast fairy had failed to visit me. Tucking the shirt into the nicest black pants I owned, I rejoined the men, looking and feeling a part of the Westside gang. What had my life become?

"Bring a lock next time." Niall nodded at my purse, which I hadn't felt comfortable enough to leave unattended in a back room. "For now, you can store it in the server section. No cell phones on the floor though, got it?"

I nodded.

"You're going to be shadowing Jasper to learn the ropes," Niall said.

My eyes flitted to Jasper.

His grin hadn't left. "My girl for the evening, eh?"

"You better be a good teacher because after today I expect to handle it all on my own. I'm a quick study." I winked at him. Whatever he was going to dish out, I was prepared to fling right back.

"I can't wait to get you on the floor."

My eyes jumped open as my heart skipped a beat. "What?"

He laughed, a warm throaty sound that bounced around me before piercing my soul. "The dining room, Sweetheart." His head nodded towards the front of the restaurant.

Niall clapped Jasper on the shoulder. "Have fun."

"Oh, we will," Jasper said, clasping my hand before I could pull away.

Electricity shot through me, tingling up my arm and setting over my chest. It put a spark into my steps.

Jasper pulled me to the serving station where he finally released my hand. "I remember you."

I stared at him, clutching my purse tightly to my chest.

"You were here with your family not so long ago." He pointed to a cubby high above the ice machine. "Put your things up there."

I reached up and tossed in my purse, hoping I would be able to grab it later. It was quite far in.

Jasper passed me a tray with a cracked edge. "You were wearing a pink sweater and your hair was tied back in a funky rope. You sat between your mom and your brother?"

I nodded slowly, unable to really believe he remembered all that. My fingers absently ran over my dark brown hair before pushing up on the edge of my glasses, moving them back into position. "My sister was home that weekend." Dina, or Geraldina as her birth certificate stated, had come home from college. She was studying at SAIT, the Southern Alberta Institute of Technology, a three-hour drive away. Nothing too far, but still enough to give her some distance from the family. And as much as she claimed she *needed* the break, she was always home at least once a month. Try as she may, it was hard to resist the pull from our family as it lured her home. It did the same with my older brother.

"I didn't notice her."

My cheeks started burning, but a smile leaked out.

"So, you've gone from the customer to the server. You know what to expect from me, now you get to be the servant."

"Sounds appealing." It was hard to keep the sarcasm from my voice as I was never one to cater to anyone's whims and desires. Instinctively I just knew I was about to get a crash course on it.

"Not really. But you can make it fun. It's all on how you play the game. Most tables are easy. Treat them nicely, and there's no fuss. It's the difficult tables that make you question your sanity. And those tables are the ones where you need to pour on the charm even more, but the reward is pretty big."

"How so?" I wrapped my arms around my tray, hugging it to my chest.

"Because some of these people come in having the shittiest day. If I can turn that around with some fun, good service and decent food, they go home and most of the time, they remember and come back."

"What?"

"Its true. I have one guy who comes here regularly, and the first time I had him, he was down on his luck, and very surly. He'd just lost his job but didn't know how to tell his wife and young children. This all came out over the course of his meal. I gave him a little more attention than my other tables, but I was mostly a sounding board. You know, someone to listen to your–"

"I know what a sounding board is."

"Oh good." Jasper smiled, the right side inched higher than the left. "Anyways, he just needed someone to hear him. At the end of his meal, I bid him good luck. He left a sizable tip, which was wrong because he should've been saving it. But you know what, he came back. Every week he comes now, always alone, but he comes. It's his private time, he tells me."

"Wow." I was shocked that someone, anyone really, took serving so seriously. "But why?"

"Why what?"

"What's in it for you?"

"Why does there need to be a pay off?" The browns of his eyes twinkled. "Maybe I just think no one should feel alone in this world. Everyone needs someone to lean on, even if it's a stranger to just hear you out. Treat them well, and you could have a customer for life."

I nearly snorted. "I have zero interest in making this a career. My goal is to get my bills paid off, save up for college and do something more with my life."

"And what is that?"

I narrowed my eyes. "I don't know yet. I'm still figuring that out." I had wavered on whether to go with earning a teaching degree or one in the child care field. I'd been approved for both, based on my high school marks. My brother thought I'd be more suited for Early Learning and Childcare, and could one day, open my own daycare. The desire to be my own boss was appealing. However, so was the idea of teaching young children. Good thing I had a few more weeks to decide as I wasn't meeting with my advisor until the end of the term, in eight weeks.

Jasper nodded. "Me too."

"Really?"

"Yeah, why are you surprised?"

"I don't know. Just thought I was the only one." I stared at him, studying the way the browns and golds twisted through his hair, wondering if his hair was soft and touchable. With my constant ogling, I almost made myself look like a complete fool. His eyes appeared older than someone my age should have, tiny little creases spread from the corners. The lines on his forehead ran parallel to his brows, but not deep enough to put him in to his thirties. But maybe?

"Hell no. I'm still trying to figure out what I want to be when I grow up." He grabbed a pen and paper from a drawer tucked under the cash register.

I could so relate to that. Real life is not astronaut training or becoming a doctor, its figuring shit out along the way. And a lot of the time it sucked. Adulting was tough. There was something to be said about remaining a kid for as long as you can. "You're not in college or university?"

"Nope. Didn't know what path I wanted to invest in for the rest of my life. Still don't." A giant smile spread across his face, creasing the wrinkles around his eyes further. "Still trying to figure out how old I am?"

"What? No." I looked down and readjusted the straps on my server apron, tightening them once again.

He leaned closer, his breath tickling my ears. "I'm twenty-three." Each syllable an ember of coal just waiting to be fanned. "But don't tell anyone."

Words failed me as I caught a whiff of his cologne. The scent turned my brain to mush. "Who… who would I tell?"

He laughed and nodded behind me. "Vernonia."

The dishwasher?

"Her English isn't great, but she flirts with me. She'd be devastated to know I'm unattainable." He winked.

I glanced toward the dish area. Vernonia was definitely older, like a mom who was saving extra for a kid's college. I didn't think she was in her twenties or even her thirties. But she was beautiful, even with her jet-black hair encased in a bright orange hairnet. She could pass for a friend of my mom's quite easily.

"Devastated, really? That much of a catch, are you?" I

laughed. Mr. Greek God had a wee bit of an ego that for some reason was highly seductive. As long as he wasn't a complete ass, we'd get a long fine.

Another server walked into the station and dropped her tray on the counter with a resounding thunk.

"Evanora, this is Shayne, the newest member of the squad."

I'd been served by Evanora once before, but I don't think she'd remembered me. She was youngish, like maybe mid-twenties, and had a warm smile, which she seemed to have left somewhere else tonight.

"Welcome. I'm assigned to L's." She sighed and filled a couple of glasses with ice, shoving them under the pop machine.

Jasper spoke to Evanora. "We'll be working in the B's, as she's training, but I could assist you if you need help."

He may have missed it, but I saw the glare she fired his way. "Not even if it was just the two of us and the line ups were an hour long." With a tray full of drinks, she walked away.

The hostess Joy who greeted me earlier, came in. "Jasper, I've sat a couple in your section."

"Thanks," he said, and passed me the pen and pad of paper. "You'll learn that there are better sections to be assigned to. Being in the b's—at the back of the restaurant—isn't ideal. The tips aren't as high at the end of the day since you don't get as many people through, but it's the perfect place to train." He started walking out of the station. "Ready to dive in and get wet?"

I matched his speed, passing the hostess station, and caught up. "Wait. You training me is going to decrease your earnings?"

"I'll make up for it with my charm. C'mon, I'll show you how this all works."

###

Evanora, Joy, Jasper, and I sat huddled in a booth after

the last customer paid and the doors were locked. It was after eleven, but the night had gone by quickly, faster than I expected.

"You did well tonight." Jasper tucked in beside me, our shoulders practically touching.

I savoured the warmth. As much as I wanted to scoot closer because the window seat where I sat was freezing, I kept myself in check. Mostly because I was afraid he'd mistake my need for heat for something more, and relationships were off the table. I didn't have time, and I most certainly wasn't ready for anything serious. I wasn't even ready for anything fun. That time would come in the fall.

"Yeah, not horrible. She only dropped one tray of drinks." Evanora laughed, ripping off the flipped over portions of her notepad, crumpling them up in her delicate palm.

"Be kind," Joy whispered and turned in my direction. "For a newbie, I'd say you were great."

One tray of four large glasses of pop equalled a restaurant silencing mess. Jasper had refilled the glasses and ran them out to the waiting table while I learned where the mop bucket was and how to clean up quickly and efficiently. Thankfully, none of the glasses broke, but still. It was quite embarrassing to happen in front of waiting crowd.

"How long before your wrists get the strength to hold a full tray?" I inquired, giving my hand a shake for effect.

"You'd be surprised. But it won't be long." Joy cracked her wrists and shrugged.

Niall walked up to the table and dropped four envelopes on it, each baring our names. "Your tips. Excellent job tonight." He looked right at me.

"Thanks," I said, my eyes falling to my envelope. It wasn't as thick as Evanora's or Joy's.

"Are you sticking around?" Niall asked me.

Was today a test? Did I miss something? "What? As in for a little longer tonight?" Westside was closed.

Jasper faced me. "Most, after their first day, abandon ship.

Decide serving's not for them."

I shook my head. "I'm good. It wasn't as bad as I expected."

Evanora grinned like Cheshire Cat, and stretched her legs out towards Niall. "It'll come."

Jasper shot her a look. "Give her a week before you start destroying her spirits."

"I'm a realist. Today wasn't crazy busy. But we're short staffed, and the busy days will be harder. Much harder." Her fingers prodded the thick envelope. "However, if you can keep them happy, the tips are great."

Jasper reached for his envelope. "That's what it's all about, right?"

"Damn straight," Evanora agreed.

Niall dropped a label maker on the table and tossed a nametag beside it.

Jasper picked it up and punched four buttons before hitting print.

"I have six letters in my name," I said, watching the label roll out of the back.

Jasper passed the raised white letters on green tape to me.

I stared at the incorrect name. "Jade?"

"Yeah. No one goes by their real name on the floor."

"Why?" I looked at Jasper's tag, and over to Evanora's and Joy's. My eyes gazed over Niall's too.

"Mine's proper, and as the manager it should be."

"Really? A fake name?"

Evanora glared in my direction. "You didn't really think my name is Evanora?"

Yeah, I did. It's beautiful and suited her. It had a nice ring to it. But I looked down.

"You're so naïve."

"Easy there," Jasper said to Evanora before he spoke to me. His tongue swiped across his full lips quickly. "It's all part of the role you're playing, Jade." As he spoke, his eyebrow flashed up and sent a crease ripping across his forehead.

"Why Jade?"

"Because you're still very green." He nodded toward Evanora. "When she started here, before the dawn of time–"

"Oh, shut up, I'm barely older than you."

"Anyways," Niall said, speaking from the head of the table. "The owner decided it was a safety issue and insisted that the front-end staff who dealt with the customers each got a nickname. It was a brilliant idea, and everyone got a work name." He placed his stubby hand on Evanora's shoulder. "She picked her name–"

"As a joke." Her eyes rolled with her words.

Niall ignored her comment, and from the way she yanked away her shoulder, I suspected there was history between them. "And suggested the others. Now it's standard and a bit of a safety issue." He grabbed the label maker and strutted back in the direction of his office.

"Safety?" A cold sweat coated the back of my neck. Until that point, I'd never worried about safety issues at work, but it made me wonder what had happened to warrant such a thing.

Waitressing wasn't that tough, was it? I didn't think the clientele was of the variety to worry about. Was it a stalker? A relationship gone wrong? At least that I could identify with.

A shiver of cold ran through me as an image I'd rather never see again flashed in my brain.

"It was before I started here," Jasper said, although he didn't follow up with how long he'd been at Westside, so it really didn't provide much information.

Another curiosity overcame me as I looked at Evanora. "What's your real name?" I could see her being a Jessica or a Victoria maybe, something elegant.

She looked me squarely in the eyes. "We're never going to be friends so there's no need to know."

Oh wow, bitch much? Maybe her real name is Bertha or Irene.

Jasper tapped his watch. "Don't you have a broom to

catch?"

She scooted out of the booth, grabbing her envelope. "Fuck off, Jasper. Goodnight." With that, she marched across the floor, and into the back, disappearing from sight.

"I'd apologize for her, but she is what she is."

I kept my mouth shut. Give her the benefit of the doubt that she wasn't a complete bitch. Besides, she did say they were short staffed, and maybe she was just tired.

I turned in Joy's direction. "So, Joy isn't your real name either?"

"Nope," she said, the 'p' strongly pronounced.

Jasper gave me my nametag. "Here you go, Jade."

The new name rolled off his tongue in perfect harmony. I could get used to being called that. I could make it fun. Wear green in my hair, I could even find a cheap pair of green frames and wear them as my work glasses.

He exited the booth and I stood beside him, unsure of what to do next or where to go. "So, do I wash floors or something?"

"No. The cleaning crew comes in about an hour. We're all done."

Joy jumped out of the booth. "Ciao, guys," her voice singing as she crossed the room. "Ride's here."

"Niall will give you your next shifts. See him before you leave."

"Aren't you leaving too?"

"I wait for Niall. Occasionally he drops me off on his way home."

I swallowed. "Where do you live?"

"That moved quick, we hardly know each other." He stepped closer to me.

I'm sure he heard the relentless pounding in my chest because it felt as if it were fluffing my shirt. "What?" There's no way I'd do that.

"We just met."

"I was just being–"

His laugh melted my heart and soothed my nerves. "I'm kidding. It's all part of the role."

I looked at him through narrowed slits. "And what role is that?"

"Playful, cocky. It's what all the women want. A self-assured man." That knowing wink stopped my heart.

I scoffed. Maybe most women did. All I wanted was someone who'd be honest with me, and not string me along. Someone who would treat me decently. That wasn't too much to ask, right? Wait, what? Why was I even thinking that, I didn't date co-workers. I looked into his waiting brown eyes and shook my head. "You don't know everything."

"I know enough that I got *you* thinking about it."

I sighed and walked into the back office. Niall handed me a schedule—all evenings, exactly what I asked for. Tucking it into my apron, I spun around and right into the hard wall of Jasper. I stumbled back. God, he felt great beneath my palms. I needed help. Serious help. And maybe a little alone time with my thoughts.

He leaned closer, his lips inches from my ears. "Don't you want to know *my* real name?"

Heat pooled in places I rather thought they shouldn't while at work, but it was totally reactionary. He was just so yum.

You're not to date people you work with. My brother's voice echoed in my head.

Damn him. I stepped back into the small row of lockers. "I don't," I whispered, my voice betraying my strength as it cracked. Inhaling a scent of musk and heady goodness, I pushed past him. "Goodnight, Jasper." I enunciated all four syllables for good measure a blast of cold, wintery air washing over me as I stepped outside.

Chapter Two

A week had passed, but I survived and held my own. Against the B section, wobbly trays *and* Jasper. The man was unrelenting with his casual comments, his flirtatious voice and his panty-soaking smile. It took everything in me to brush him off. Even if it was *just an act,* it was still very convincing. Truly, the Academy Award was his. And I'd like to deliver it.

Even though we all wore the same standard uniform, something about the way he wore his fired up my insides. Maybe it was the bulge in his arms, or the way the polo was tucked into the waist of the black pants or the way he tied his leftover apron strings into a bow rather than a knot. Whatever it was, he was hard to not watch. And I found myself watching him from all angles. Constantly. Every shift. All shift long.

It was after eight, and the crowds had thinned to a trickle. The supper rush had been crazy busy, but I'd managed on my own taking a max of three tables at a time. My latest table just arrived. Four adults, all ordering coffee. Why not? It was brutally cold, and I would've had something warm as well. Not coffee, because that's gross, maybe a hot chocolate or something.

I grabbed three mugs from the shelf and set them on my tray. A quick glance to the machine. A half pot sat on top, and a full, fresh one sat on the bottom. I reached for the needed fourth mug with my left hand and gripped the half-empty pot on top with my right. As I lifted it off the heating element, an ear-shattering crack splintered the air as the bottom of the coffee pot burst apart. Hot coffee sprayed all over my left hand. Instinctively I dropped the mug, and it crashed onto the floor.

"Son-of—" but the rest of the words were muted.

Jasper's hand had been quick to cover it. "Easy there, sailor. There are children nearby." As quickly as he uncovered my mouth, he had the faucet beside me running and my scalding, hurting hand thrust under the cool water. The contrast between the two was borderline excruciating, and I bit my lip to keep from saying as much.

"Is there glass in your hand?" His voice was soft and surprisingly calm.

I shook my head. It didn't feel like there was. It only felt burnt.

His tender hand ran over my reddened palm, soft leather against my sandpaper. Mesmerized, I watched unable to tear my eyes away. I blinked away the moisture forming.

"Are you okay?"

My gaze moved up to his piercing browns; unbridled concern registered in them.

I nodded. But I didn't know if I really was. My hand screamed at me, despite the cool of the water and the warmth of his hand caressing the top of my scalded skin. My legs trembled, and I worried they'd give out. I wasn't the strongest person when it came to things like this. In fact, I became very childlike in my dependency on someone else to take control—when there was another older person who could. It was a wonder I'd managed to live on my own for a year without disaster striking. Completely anyway.

So, I allowed him to take over. I gave him the reins.

Like an expert, he held my hand under the steady stream of cool.

"Watch your step," Jasper said to Evanora as she entered the server station.

"Oh shit," Evanora said. "Another one?" She grabbed the broom and swept the mess, shards of coffee pot mixed with brown liquid, off to the side so no one would immediately step in it. The *Slippery When Wet* sign came out and she set up on the other side of me. "Watch your step," she told me, as if I was an idiot.

The shaking deepened, but I was pretty sure it was because of the chilly water.

Jasper pushed his shoulder against me and I was relieved to have something to lean on. The arm touching me was warm. How was that possible? He had his hand in the water just as much as mine.

"This is the second pot in a month to burst. I'm starting to think we got a bad shipment or something." His hand continued to stroke mine, and goosebumps pimpled my fleshy arms. "It's nothing you did, in case you were wondering."

I wasn't, but thanks.

"How's your hand doing?"

It wasn't hurting so much. I pulled it out of the stream.

"Not just yet. Leave it there for a minute." Drying his hands, he reached over my head and pulled down an emergency kit. The lid open, he retrieved a sealed package of rolled up bandages. "Okay." He grabbed a clean cloth from the shelving atop the coffee station, and gingerly, as if he held fine china, wrapped it around my hand. With the gentlest of squeezes, he patted dry my cooled down hand. Parts of it were speckled white, a deep contrast to the crimson red over most of my hand and on my wrist.

The smell of burnt coffee permeated my nose, and I wiggled it in disgust.

With his elbow, Jasper flicked the off switch on the machine. "I'll clean that in a bit." His eyes never left mine, and somehow, I felt safe in them. A gob of yellow goo squeezed out of a white tube. Delicately, he rubbed it over the worst of the red marks. He wrapped the roll of gauze around my palm, keeping it snug but not too much, and tucked the end in. Lifting it up to his mouth, he placed a kiss atop my one exposed knuckle.

Breaking the spell between us, he tipped his head toward my tray of three mugs, a half inch of coffee and broken glass swimming around them. "What table?"

I blinked. I'd long since forgotten there had even been customers. "Umm…" A flash to the group of four. "B9."

He squeezed my shoulder. "I'll inform them about the situation." A fresh coffee pot appeared, and I watched with rapt attention as he ripped open a fresh bag of grounds and dumped them unceremoniously into the filter. Filling four new mugs, all placed on the tray first, he took off toward my table.

I grabbed the broom, but the handle from it pushed against the covered part on my hand, and pain radiated out. Taking a deep breath, I bit through it, sweeping up the pushed out of the way shards and as little liquid I could. My shoes took a bit of the mess, although I guessed with the thick material and my socks, it was unlikely that they burned. My legs didn't even feel wet. Dumping the dust pan, I resumed cleaning up the mess. I even dried the area with paper towels so that the sign could be tucked away, along with my embarrassment.

Jasper was by my side as I finished up. "Looking good."

"Well, it's dry," I said, surveying the area. It was still messy, but a good mop would be able to make it spic and span clean.

"I meant you."

My cheeks singed, and likely matched the color of my hand. At least that was hidden beneath a thick wrap of bandages. I straightened up and turned away, patting my pocket to double check my paper and pen were still there when I spotted Evanora advancing toward me.

"I just sat a couple in your section." Her voice ripe with disgust. "You two need to be out there on the floor, not hanging out back here." With a sharp turn, she disappeared.

"Pleasant, isn't she?"

"Just part of the act, right?"

"If you want to believe that, then yes." He shrugged and filled a couple of glasses with ice.

I stepped closer to him, the heat in my cheeks cooling, but the pounding in my chest increased tenfold with each inch. "Thank you for the first aid."

"Thank you for not swearing."

"You're like Superman."

"Only until I see my kryptonite."

"And that would be?" I rose my eyebrow in questioning.

"Perhaps someday you'll find out."

"Can you answer me a question?"

He turned his full attention my way, the overhead lights absorbing into the dark dreads on his head, the tips turning a light brown. Those intensity-filled eyes took me in, in a personal way, in a way you knew just by looking, that the man behind the eyes was kind and honest. That part of him wasn't an act.

"I want to know what your real name is, although Jasper suits you."

The distance between us gone, his face was close enough to feel the whiskers on his cheeks as they brushed against mine. I closed my eyes and breathed him in, my heart pounding against my rib cage. Every fiber of my being was alive and roaring, something about his presence setting it all on fire.

His voice a whisper, the words danced in my ear. "Korey."

Chapter Three

I sat atop one of two available padded vinyl seats in a crowded section of *Laugh 'N Play*, a giant warehouse filled with climbing structures and play spaces for children of all ages. Leaning on a length of table top space beside my best friend, Lily, we kept our eyes on the children. Her youngest daughter played in the area I affectionately called *the pen*; a play space where babies and toddlers could climb over padded blocks and slide down miniature slides, safely enclosed from the big kids who ran, pushed and screamed behind them.

"I swear, I thought this place would be less busy today," Lily said, glaring at a big kid who cursed at his friend.

"It's probably a PD day or something, because yeah, there aren't normally big kids here at ten on a school day."

"Damn Professional Days." Lily swiped her mahogany hair off her face and sighed. The circles under her eyes were darker than normal, no doubt due to a lack of sleep as she'd been up most of the night nursing her sick husband through his cold. Man cold, that's what she called it.

Regardless, she was still beautiful, in my opinion. A nice person on the inside, someone I'd come to cherish as a true friend. Twelve years my senior, she had a wealth of parenting advice I thrived off. Her tips were invaluable in my training, as currently I was a nanny to a precious little three-year-old boy.

I sort of fell into the job on a full-time basis. When I called the number listed in the newspaper, I'd accidentally dialled the number in the ad above. The ad I thought I was calling about was for a spring break babysitting job. I learned at the interview this was not the case and by the end of the hour-long meet and greet, I'd met Jordan, and fallen in love with the precocious child. The rest, as they say, was history.

I've been with Jordan for over a year, and he's like a son to me. Except at three o'clock, when he went back to his mother, Aimee, and I headed home to change into Westside clothing. Aimee's hours had been reduced at her job, and with it, my own hours by default. I found myself scrambling to pay rent. She never paid much, but it was enough. Until recently. Plus, she left money for incidentals like hot chocolate and the play park, and that's how I met Lily. Her daughter and 'my son' were a month apart in age.

"How's the new job?" Lily asked and searched the area for her daughter.

"She's by the slide," I said. "With Jordan." I twisted in my seat and rested my elbows on the ledge. "The job is good. Late nights though. This working until eleven every night, and then waking to be at his house by eight is taxing."

"I thought you only worked a couple of shifts a week?"

"Five evenings, actually. Wednesday through Sundays."

"Shit, girl." Lily rummaged through her ginormous diaper bag and pulled out a wet wipe. In one smooth motion, she'd washed our tiny corner of the counter.

"Well the tips are good. I figure at this pace, I'll be caught up on bills by the end of next month. Then I'll be able to set some money aside if I budget properly." I scanned the area when Jordan disappeared for a moment. *Found him.* He was trying to stack the foam blocks.

"I admire you. I couldn't do it."

I twisted in my seat, swinging my legs like a child. "But you do. What with Jason's cold and the three girls. You're working harder than I do, and you're not getting paid for it."

"And what about college? How are you going to manage

that in the fall?"

I dusted the crumbs off the bar-like table. "Well, that will come with a bit of juggling, but we'll see how it goes. For now, my plan is to go to class full-time, and work part-time in the evenings, at Westside most likely."

"That'll keep you busy."

"Hopefully not too busy." I smiled and tipped my head down. "I plan on experiencing the full college life. Parties. Late nights. The social scene. Cramming for finals. Living off caffeine. Everything."

"Ah, the college movie. You don't want real-life, you want the fantasy."

I blinked rapidly. Lily had always been blunt with me, it was something I liked about her. Straight to the point, no beating around the bush. But at that moment, I didn't want her honesty. I wanted her to agree that it sounded like fun.

"What happens when the bubble bursts? Then what?"

Another quick scan of the play area. Jordan was still playing with the blocks and building a nice tower. "If the bubble bursts, then I go back to being boring old Shayne, lonely keeper of the books. But if I am going to live the fantasy, as you call it, then I'm going to have to put myself out there. Be adventurous and try new things."

"You're going to do that?"

I shrugged. "Why not?"

"I don't believe it. You're too much of a homebody. You're not the partying kind."

The hell I wasn't. I went to a party not so long ago. It was a New Year's party. At my brother's house. Okay, fine, point taken. That was over a couple months back. And aside from Lily, I didn't have any real friends.

Relationships were hard for me. Between not being popular enough in high school to hang with the cool kids, or being into sports to hang with the jocks, I roved – moving from group to group not sure where to fit in. Not into art, and not into the whole conformity thing that came with being a goth, I tried hanging out with the nerds. Except the nerds deemed me not smart enough, so I became an outcast. And was happy there. All alone. Just me and my school work and endless supplies of books. The librarian became my friend.

Don't even get me started on boyfriends. Since I wasn't 'easy', and the guys who did talk to me told me I'd likely need the assistance of the jaws of life, boyfriends were as few and far between as friends. My last boyfriend, the guy I'd been with for a while, had done a number on me as my brother-in-law liked to say, and I'd been exceptionally careful about letting new people into my life ever since.

Jordan pushed a little girl who was bigger than him after she kicked down his tower.

"Ah, crap." I jumped into the pit and kneeled to his height. "Now, Jordan, that wasn't very nice."

"She wheked my tower."

"I know, but that doesn't give you the right to be mean to her. You're allowed to be sad or mad, but you can't be mean." I held his hand and cupped his chin in my hand, looking him directly in the eye. "You need to apologize to her."

"Your son pushed my little girl," a stern voice hovered over me.

I stood and stared down at her. "I'm aware of what he did, and I'm dealing with that. However, your little angel instigated it when she kicked over the tower."

"She fell."

God, they were all the same. Always somebody else's fault. No responsibility. "I watched her do it. There was no falling." I pulled Jordan close. Some mothers truly believed their children could do no wrong, and she clearly fell into that camp.

"She fell."

I rolled my eyes. "I refuse to get into a battle with you over this. I know what I saw. I will deal with my child, and I suggest you parent your own." I turned my attention back to

Jordan, where it deserved to be. Somehow, I just knew the ignorant woman was shooting daggers at me. The back of my head hurt. "Jordan, what do you say?"

Jordan stood grim-faced in front of the little girl. "Sorry." It was the feeblest apology ever.

"Thank you, Jordan." I walked him back over to our spot and as soon as he climbed up on my stool, the incident behind him was long forgotten. Oh, to be a child and to never hold on to the anger. Just bam, deal with it and move on. There was a lesson in there somewhere. I just wasn't sure how to apply that to real life.

I pulled out a baggie of grapes and passed it to Jordan. I'd said my peace and discussing it with him now was fruitless.

Lily seemed unphased of the whole situation and took a long swig of her coffee. "Any new men on the frontier?"

I laughed. "Yeah right. Men are bad news, remember?" Naivety was my weakness, but also my greatest teacher. I learned that some men are born jerks, and I had no desire to walk that path anytime soon. Not even with Korey, even if most of my dreams and personal time had been Korey-centric lately. Not that it meant much, aside from the fact I couldn't get him out of my mind. Besides, dating work mates always spelled trouble.

"Well, it's not like you'd have time with all this working, for dating anyways. And it's over rated. Look what happens when you fall in love." She sniffed her daughter's bottom. "Man colds and shitty diapers."

Lily was so funny, if not slightly jaded. I guess being a full-time mom did that sometimes. "Think of all the cuddles and unconditional love."

"Says the one who gives the child back to its owner. You miss out on all the fun stuff." She rolled her eyes. "Puking kids at three am, nightmares, attitudes." Lily grabbed the diaper bag. "I'll be back."

"I'll keep watch on the other two." When Lily walked out of sight, I gave Jordan a kiss on his little forehead. "Grown ups, eh?" I ruffled his hair and stole a grape.

Chapter Four

A month into waitressing, and I had a firm handle on what I was supposed to do. I was no longer training, thank god, but managing my own sections with finesse and minimal spillage. I'd even successfully gone two weeks without hurting myself, the last being the nasty burn incident.

Korey, or Jasper as his work nametag said, was still relentless in his pursuit. Whether it was merely a game to him or not, I wasn't sure as I couldn't read between the lines. He didn't seem to be as sweet to the other co-workers except maybe the dish washer. There was certainly no love towards Evanora, and I wondered if they'd been boyfriend-girlfriend once. Their attitudes toward each other spoke volumes, I just wasn't sure if it was the right volume.

With another shift under my belt, I sat in what was referred to as the staff booth. After locking up, it was where we sat and unwound, and received any tip money that had been left on credit cards. The cash tips we pocketed right away as we cleaned the table. I tucked tonight's envelope into my apron pocket.

I was so close to being able to get my credit card paid off. So close. At this rate, in two more payments it should be done. A hard lesson to learn when I racked up my Visa and only made the minimum payments. My dad said everyone made that mistake at some point and offered to help me pay off the huge amount, but

I figured it would be a better lesson to do it on my own. After all, I'd made the mistake, and I needed to take responsibility for it.

As per usual, Jasper sat beside me, super close. Close enough that I could breathe him in, all spice and musk. Joy, aptly named as she was seriously the happiest person ever, sat across from us. I envied Joy and her outlook on life. Everything was truly sunshine and roses with her, but because of what I knew about Jasper, I wondered if it was an act. And if it was, she was fantastic at hiding any pain or sadness. I wish I could be as solid as that.

"It's so good to be back," she said, stretching her long, lean arms above her head. "Don't ever get your tonsils removed. It's simply murder on the throat." All said with a smile as she popped a lozenge into her mouth. "But I did get lots of love and care."

"It's much more pleasant closing with you again." Jasper held his envelope in his hands, flipping it over and over. He nudged me a couple of times. Accidentally I thought. Or maybe on purpose since he did it more than once.

Joy straightened herself up and waved her hand in a mock slap. "Oh stop, Evanora's going through a lot."

"Whatever," he said.

Joy inched herself toward us, leaning far over the green table top. "I overheard her talking into her phone about her kid and how she had to come home immediately as he was sick. She was scrambling to find another sitter on short notice."

"What?" Aside from the fact Evanora didn't look old enough to be a mother, I had to jump in. I couldn't imagine telling Aimee that I wasn't going to watch Jordan because he was ill. On those days, I simply took extra precautions and doubled up on my vitamins and triple washed my hands. Those days also came with extra snuggles and extra doses of kid cartoons. It was kind of tough to turn down, and I sometimes felt bad for Aimee knowing she was missing out on that with her own kid. Then again, Lily said she got more than enough. "Maybe I could help her out?"

"She works evenings, just like you." Jasper gave me a

blank look. "And I need you on my shifts." It was quick, but his hand graced mine. "I want you on my shifts."

"Right." Since I was needed here, it would be impossible to be in two places at once.

Joy's phone buzzed, and a larger smile spanned across her face as she looked at the screen. "Gotta run. My man's parked outside. G'nite all." She danced across the floor, waving her goodbyes to the staff still tidying up in the kitchen.

Jasper cleared his throat and pushed against my shoulder. "Well, it's a Friday night. What are your big plans?"

"Honestly?" I unbuttoned the top button on my shirt. "I'm going home to curl up with a good read." If I made it beyond the first couple of chapters of the newest Sarah J. Maas read. My feet ached, and I was worn out, so it was the perfect way to end the day.

He scrunched up his brows and smirked. "You sure you're nineteen? You're like the oldest nineteen-year-old I've ever met. "

"Because it'll be nearly eleven when I get home? I've been up since six." My hands pushed against his upper body, scooting him out of the booth.

He stood and left me no room to sneak on by. "Well, that and because you're going home to read. It's a Friday night."

"What's wrong with that?" Again, I nudged his firm body out of the way and stood beside the booth.

"What are you reading?"

With that, I raised my brows. "Do you really want to know, or do you just want to shame me?"

"Oooh, shame you? Okay, now I'm super curious about your book of choice. What could little miss goody two-shoes be reading?" He rubbed the whiskers on his chiseled chin and glanced up at the overhead lights.

"Goody two-shoes?" Ugh, it was high school all over again. Labelled as someone who couldn't be fun.

His gaze, calm and steady, returned to lock on me. "Yeah.

You don't come across as a girl who likes to party."

That will change in the fall. I hoped. My calendar would be so full, I'd be tired from that, not from the hours of studying and working. "Depends on the party." He didn't need to know my lack of attendance at decent parties.

He crossed his arms over his chest. "Do you prefer the wild, drinking and dancing type of parties, or the more intimate type? Like a getting to know you kind?"

Personally, it was the latter. Bad things happened when the drinking got out of hand, so I'd never partake in that. However, I enjoyed the energy of a crowd of dancing people. The couple of times I'd gone.

A yawn slipped out and I covered it quickly.

"Time for you to go home and read and catch some zzz's." He gave my shoulder a little squeeze and a pat, and his tongue swiped across his lips.

Seeing that wet, dark pink flicker fired up a carnal burning in me. Maybe a bath with some silky bath oil and a little getting to know myself time was in order. "Yeah, that sounds sweet. I've been chasing after a three-year-old all day, and then I came in and played nice with customers. I'm exhausted."

As if he'd be tasered, his hand snapped off me and he stepped back. "Three-year-old?" The sweetness he once held on his face melted off.

My heart pounded, and anger rose sharply within. I toyed between the idea of being honest about Jordan rather than letting him think that Jordan was my kid. Honesty won out; like always. "I'm a nanny during the day."

His eyes narrowed. "Aren't you a little young to be a Mary Poppins?"

I couldn't help myself, the way he phrased it and the confused look on his face made me laugh. People always referred to that damn Poppins lady whenever I told them what I did, but coming from him? For whatever reason I got the giggles. "Supercalifragilisticexpialidocious." I put a hop into my walk as I sang the rest of the lyrics.

"For real?" He followed me to the staff change area.

"It's even my fake name while I'm there. Jordan refers to me as Nanny Poppins." It was a total lie, but it was fun to egg him on. "But only until the next gust of wind carries me away." To college.

"Wow. You're really–"

"What? Old?" I beat him to the punch.

"No, what I was going to say was…" He paused and studied me, his eyes raking up and down my body.

I didn't want to hear what it was he thought of me. My good mood gone, and all the carnal feelings snuffed out in a heartbeat, I stomped to the staff change area, grabbing my jacket and purse.

Jasper hadn't followed but at the back entrance reserved only for deliveries and letting the night shift out, he leaned against one side of the doorway, his muscular arm braced against the other side.

"Get out of my way."

He smirked. "Absolutely not."

I ducked under and pushed against the door. Unsurprisingly, the heavy metal door didn't move.

"Let's talk."

"So you can make more assumptions?"

"So I can get to know you. You're so not what I pictured."

"I don't care." I pushed against the door again. It was fruitless, but still. I was trying to make my point.

Jasper looked unfettered. A small grin played on those lips, and if he kept looking at me like that, I'd have to fight a lot harder to walk away. A sad little pout curled out his bottom lip. "Why don't you want to talk to me?"

"I talk to you all the time."

He chuckled, a low throaty sound that caused my core to roar with desire. "I want to know about you." A long finger grazed my cheek and tucked a loose strand of dark hair behind the arm of my glasses.

"I don't date co-workers." It was the dumbest thing to say, but I couldn't think of anything else.

The acorn-coloured flecks in his irises twinkled as the grin became a broad smile, pushing up the corners of his eyes. "Who said anything about dating?"

"Umm, no one. I just wanted to be clear on that." I tried to hide the quivering in my voice, but I'm pretty sure I failed miserably. Jasper was unknowingly setting my body on fire, and I needed to desperately get away from him, go home and put those fires out. On my own. I couldn't even look at him. Radiant sex god that he was. He probably knew it too.

The air crackled with the hum of the overhead lights. Neither of us moved for several heartbeats.

He continued to take me in, his smile never wavering and with it, my imagination took flight in a wildly seductive way, replacing the main character in my latest romance read with him. I imagined myself pulling his form-fitting green top out of the waistband of his black pants and running my fingers over his body. I wondered if he was hairless or sported a chest full. A quick glance to the vee in the polo neck, failed to reveal anything. Maybe he was smooth chested. Not that it mattered. The temperature rose in my body, and the heat wiggled its way up to my cheeks.

Finally, he cleared his voice and spoke softly, "I thought you wanted to go?"

I knew it was stupid, and it was nine shades crazier than anything I'd done before, but I couldn't help myself. I needed to know if the lustful feeling was reciprocated as he got me all hot and bothered. Did I do the same to him or was it all a game? Before I could stop myself and allow sensibility to control me, I kissed him. Hard and with more passion and excitement than I would've ever admitted.

And when he wrapped his arms around me and pushed back into the kiss, I knew I was a goner.

###

I barely had the apartment door locked before I tossed my coat on the floor and kicked my shoes into the corner. Korey mirrored my actions and picked me up where I wrapped my legs around him like a boa constrictor. I ran my fingers through the parts of his hair I felt I safely could. The dreads were not what I expected, the ropes of hair soft against my palm. My lips found his, and my tongue probed the depths of his mouth. I couldn't keep my hands still, probably because my heart pounded so fiercely against my ribs. Crushed up against him, I had no doubt he could feel it too.

Fumbling our way in the dark and down the short hall, he found my bedroom and dropped me on my bed. I landed on a bag of used toys I'd bought for Jordan and rolled off, kicking the bag onto the floor.

Korey reached for the hem of his shirt.

"Oh please." I begged and scrambled up onto my knees. "Let me." Everything I'd imagined came to life as I slipped under the shirt and felt the smoothest, yet softest skin. Beneath the chill of my hand, his body rippled and tightened, and I lifted the shirt up.

Korey yanked it off before I could tease him further, and a green puddle of fabric hit the floor. His breath was quick as I licked up his chest and found his lips again.

His fingers danced down my back, synapses firing up with each touch. In one smooth motion, my own polo shirt easily flew off my body, leaving me in a ratty, but still doing its job, bra. The bright amethyst colour had long since washed out and at its best could be considered lavender. Thank god it was dark, and he couldn't tell. Had I known how my day would end…

Fingers that had held my hands, now ran up my arms, hooking my bra straps and slipping them slowly, gently, to the point of heady anticipation, over my shoulders. His breathy kisses moved down my chin, over the curve of my neck and tingled as he traced a wanton path toward the tops of my arms. It was enough to make me explode right then and there.

I couldn't breathe. It was mesmerizing and intoxicating.

For hours, words escaped us. Our lips silenced the other, preferring plenty of sensuous lip to heated skin contact. There was enough to make my heart pound fearlessly, and my breath to catch repeatedly as he stroked and caressed the woman out of me.

Multiple times.

Being with Korey was unlike anything I'd ever encountered and as schooled as I was in the intimacy department, he taught me so much more. How to give up myself and surrender to the feelings of pure ecstasy, the kind you only get naturally. There would never be a drug to make someone feel so desired, and wanted, and to a small degree, loved. And when I started to sense that from him, I checked out and yawned.

# # #

Awaking in the morning as my alarm sounded, I was more than a little surprised to see Korey still in my bed, sure he would've left at some point during the night. I shifted through the clothes on the floor, and not finding what I was looking for, pulled the comforter off my bed. I'd need to remake it anyway with clean sheets.

"Hey," he said, sleep lining his voice.

"Morning."

"Helluva night, eh?"

I nodded. I didn't want to get into specifics, but yeah, it was a great night. He's as strong as he appeared, and he appeared very fit and muscular. I'd never had sex standing up, and certainly not while being lifted. My Adonis was Thor strong and as bendable as Gumby.

As that mixture of images circled my head, I laughed.

"What's so funny?"

"My room is a disaster," I said, glancing around at the

strewn clothing everywhere. *Was that his underwear on my lamp?* I shook my head and grabbed some fresh clothes. "I'm taking a shower. Feel free to help yourself to food in the kitchen."

Part of me, a huge part if I were going to be honest with myself, hoped he'd be gone when I got out of the bathroom thirty minutes later. I'd chalk this encounter up to a one-time thing and hope it wouldn't affect our working relationship. A smaller part of me, the one that hoped he'd stay at least for a little bit, won.

He sat at my kitchen table, as tiny as it was, eating a bowl of cereal. I shuddered to think how stale that was; I'd bought it before Christmas. Did cereal retain its freshness for four months?

"You said to help myself." How he managed to look so perfect after that night, baffled me. Maybe that was the magic of dreads and the start of a beard, but it always looked sexy. However, he was in his work clothes from last night, so the walk of shame still stretched out before him.

"I did." I knew there wasn't much too munch on, so I scooped out a small bowl of yogurt and sprinkled my homemade topping on it. Unsure if I should join him at the table or just eat it where I stood, I twisted my spoon in the bowl, taking an unusual amount of time to decide.

Korey brought his dish to the sink, and wash and dried it. "Are you going to eat?"

"Thinking about it." I twirled my spoon more, burying it beneath a strawberry morsel, refusing to make eye contact. *What did he think of me now? Was I a slut for sleeping with him? Would this be it? Or would he want more? Did I even want more?* Holding the bowl, I walked away from Korey's intense stare down and sat at the table.

"About last night," he said, his voice getting stronger as he closed in on me and the table. "I remember what you said."

I stared at him trying to remember what specifically I had said. There weren't a lot of words exchanged. Some praying, maybe, but I didn't think that's what he referred to.

"About how you don't date co-workers?"

I nodded. That I remembered. A quick glance to the

clock. Remembering I'd agreed to help my sister unpack, I realised there wouldn't be time for a long in-depth discussion. I hoped he'd make this quick. But he looked at me for an explanation, so I supposed I should lead off.

"Here's the thing, Korey. Last night was a one-time thing. Something sparked between us and we extinguished it. I don't need things awkward between us at work. Like at all." I wanted to believe that it truly was a one-time thing, but I knew better because hope lingered nearby. I hoped to touch that magnificent body again. I hoped to connect with him as it was a great release to the day.

However, I didn't want a commitment, didn't want to be tied down. I wasn't looking for that right now and didn't need it. Maybe most girls my age did, but that didn't make it right. I was happy on my own and had been for a long while. Yes, it had been hard to get my bearings straight after the whole Ben incident, but I managed. On my own.

Plus, college loomed on the horizon and I had big plans to party and make friends. College was meant for new experiences, not for being tied down to a boyfriend. My life was tied down enough right now with two full-time jobs. Dating any more than at a casual level was not in my cards. Oh man, my brother was so right on workplace relationships. I hadn't even started one and look at me. A sigh breathed out from me.

"I hear ya." He grabbed the kitchen chair and spun it around, straddling it. "About dating co-workers."

Oh, how badly I wanted to be that chair. To be straddled.

Korey snapped his fingers in front of my face. "And you know what, I don't get involved with co-workers either."

Not sure why, but I didn't really believe that. I gave him a questionable look. "Oh, really?"

"Are you referring to Evanora and I?" Evanora's name spit from his mouth like venom.

"Yeah, you two act like you've had a hookup or two." Or a serious relationship gone sideways.

"Absolutely never." He shook his head and rested his chin on his arms. "Never, ever. The only time I've ever been remotely smitten with anyone I've ever worked with is... You." Those deep brown eyes bored into my soul.

"Me?"

"Yeah."

The clock ticked loudly beside me, it's metronome-like beat clashing against the rushing of blood pulsing through my veins. "But you two seem to have a chemistry?"

He laughed. "Like a ticking time-bomb."

"Would you ever... do her?"

He tipped his head to the side. "Don't get me wrong, Evanora's beautiful. But she's a bitch. Probably in the middle of a hot night of passion she'd complain I was doing it wrong and make me start over."

I giggled because that would be funny to watch, but I was a wee bit jealous. As much as he claimed he wasn't interested in her, he had thought about her in a sexual way.

"Forget about her. I do."

I nodded, unsure if I truly bought the story he was selling. "How can we make..." His eyebrow raised seductively, and I lost my train of thought. "Make this work?" My hands twisted together. "If we keep hooking up, can we keep it a secret?" And hook-ups were only a temporary thing, right? Like, this could all be over in a month?

"Because it was so secret last night?"

Oh shit, right. We were lip-locked at the back door for a long time. I'm sure the entire staff saw us. Well maybe half, but you know what I meant. "Well?"

"Why is it so important?"

"Because I need this job. I need the money. College isn't free, and it most definitely isn't cheap. I'm going in the fall, and the only way I can get there is by saving up. All my savings disappeared."

"Disappeared? How?"

A large lump appeared in my throat. "I'm …" My gaze went everywhere but his face. "I'm not ready to discuss that." I swallowed down my self-pity. Ben and I had worked together on the weekends at the car lot and after everything went down, I quit. I had to. There were too many questions and wandering eyes to avoid. "So, if we can't keep this from being a thing, then I'll have to quit."

"I'm not following you."

"Look, Korey, we become an item and things go south and we break up, work becomes a personal hell, even if one likes doing the job."

"You're speaking in hypotheticals."

"It's my specialty."

"Well…" He rubbed his chin and cocked his head. "Let's take it one day at a time. Last night was a little unusual for me."

"Which part?" I doubted it was the sex, because that was… well, passionate and exciting. There was no winging that part or any of it, really. It was perfection. Mind and body blowing perfection.

"I'll let your imagination run wild with that." He rose and tucked in his chair. "That being said, I'd like to take you out for a proper afternoon date, since we work tonight. May I?"

Dammit. I shook my head, thankful I had a valid excuse. "I'm helping my sister move into her boyfriend's apartment."

"Thought she lived in Calgary?"

"She did, until yesterday. She's on her way up right now, and I'm supposed to meet her at her boyfriend's apartment in twenty minutes."

"Can I help?"

How would my family react to him? Not that I was afraid of that, but I'd never mentioned Korey to anyone aside from my brother and even that was just talk that nothing had happened or was going to happen. If Korey showed up, I'd have to eat my words.

Chapter Five

Eating my words sucked.

With more hesitation than I should have, given he'd offered to help a perfect stranger move, I handed Korey the address of the apartment my sister was moving into.

I parked my car on the street and barely had time to send a text message to Lily before I spotted him. Striding toward me from the parking lot, he looked showered and preened, like he'd had all morning to clean up. Dudes have it so much easier. I would've taken an hour to look as good as him.

Inhaling a sharp breath, I swallowed my fear of the impending situation, and headed over to the giant U-Haul, trying to keep a casual distance between Korey and me.

It was easy to spot my sister, just based on sound. Her loud voice carried above the small gathering of people around her as she barked out orders about how she marked the boxes and labeled all the rooms in the apartment to make it easier on everyone.

I rolled my eyes and smirked in Korey's direction. He seemed unfettered and kept pace with me. Just wait until she gave him the order of the boxes she wanted unpacked first. Seriously, OCD does not even begin to explain my sister.

"Shayne," she yelled as she spotted me and stole a peek at her watch. "Glad you could make it on time." Always with the snark.

"I'm like five minutes late."

"Who's this?" she asked, breaking away from the small crowd.

The group contained my parents, my older brother Sean and his husband, Randy, Xander and a few other guys I didn't recognize, probably friends of Xander's. However, it was my family's glare that froze me in my tracks. They weren't judging per se, but they had curious looks on their faces directed at the man beside me.

"This is Korey and he figured you could use another set of hands and gladly volunteered his services." I wanted to pat his chest with my hand but restrained myself. As far as everyone in the vicinity knew, we were strictly friends, and I intended to make sure that appearance stuck. Behind the sanctity of my own door, we could be the wild animals we were last night.

"Korey," my sister said and gave him a solid once over. "Why do I recognize you?"

I knew exactly what her tone implied, but I wasn't going to give in. Not here in front of my father's intense stare. Not until I had a chance to talk to Randy and Sean first. Not really until I was sure of the whole thing myself. "He works with me at Westside."

"Ah, that's why. Well…" She clapped her hands and turned back towards her help. "This shouldn't take long then. Boxes are marked, start with the highest number please. Rooms are marked to match the boxes. Let's get moving." She fist-bumped an imaginary friend and passed out the first box.

I headed to the back of the U-Haul. Korey stood and stared, and I understood why. The boxes were not just numbered but each contained a few sentences of description. Surely, *kitchen* would've been enough? But no, my sister had *Kitchen box #20, utensils. Place on counter, not on floor. Open third.*

My sister was organized to a tee. It's almost a problem *how* organized she was. I've never moved with the efficiency she packed into this move, and I couldn't even begin to figure out how she planned it so well. I supposed that's why it took me a full day to move into my apartment, not like the hour it took to move her. Surprising really at how fast it all went, even moving everything to the third-floor apartment. There were a lot of stairs, as there was no elevator, but the guys all survived.

Dina decided the ladies shouldn't carry boxes, even though I would've preferred that to option A. She wanted help unpacking the kitchen, since those were the first boxes moved, according to her mile-long list. But nothing I did worked for her, and I even opened them up in the right order. Regardless, she kept moving whatever I put away, so I gave up and unpacked the bathroom, which in my opinion, was very functional when I flattened the fifteenth box.

Besides, I wasn't in the mood to gossip about Korey or provide her all the intel she wanted. Not when my mother stood five feet away and still believed I'm a virgin. That ship sailed long ago, and it would turn her remaining dark hairs white to find out *how* long ago. Some things just weren't worth sharing.

Leaving my mother and sister to continue fighting over the exact proper arrangement of the cupboards, I found Korey downstairs hanging out with the guys, fitting in like the last piece of a family-sized puzzle. I hung by the back door and peered through the window. He was perfectly at ease, laughing with the guys and swigging back a cold one. The way he smiled at Sean, you'd figure they'd known each other for years, not an hour.

"There's my girl," my dad said when he spotted me. So much for hanging back and taking in the moment.

"Hey," I said, joining the guys. "Mom and Dina are going crazy about the proper placement of the dinner plates verses the side plates, and if the bowls should rest on those, so I left. But the bathroom's done."

"Those two should open their own organizing business. They'd drive people crazy." Dad drowned his last words with a sip of beer.

My dad got me and knew it's better to walk away from

their chaos than it was to engage with it. "Just keep me out of it." I looked at the other guys standing there. "Anything else to move?"

"It's all good," Xander said, handing me my own bottle of brew. "Just need to sweep it out and take back the truck. Your friend was a great help. It screwed up Dina's original plans, but we figured it out."

I laughed and tipped the neck of my beer bottle in his direction. "You have to live with her."

"Yes, I do." Xander beamed, the look of pure love filling his face. Although I knew they were shacking up repeatedly in Calgary, between her dorm room and his off-campus place, now it was official. They now had one place to call their own.

Korey nodded and took another swig. "It was fairly easy. I may have to adopt Dina's moving regime. She seems to know what she's doing as I've never moved so quickly. And I've moved many times."

"It could be that there are also eight men moving things and only a U-Haul's worth of stuff." I pointed out.

"You'd never know that when you see *box #25 bedroom. Please set near closet*."

I laughed. As an outsider, it had to be ridiculous and bordering on the edge of insanity. It certainly was as an insider.

Korey wasn't mocking her, but it sounded funny. It was even funnier when the others joined in, calling out the box numbers they moved and their rightful descriptive locations.

I gave Korey a gentle, friendly nudge. "Look at you go, blending all in, like family."

He winked and took a long pull on the bottle.

"Let's finish our beers." Xander reached into the case at his feet and offered out another bottle to anyone needing one. "And head back upstairs. Knowing Dina, she'll have lunch ordered and we can feed all you hard-working souls."

Twisting off the cap, I put the bottle to my lips and chugged back the first few tastes. It was really the only part of a beer I enjoyed. After that, it usually remained untouched.

"Are you staying for lunch?" I asked Korey as he finished up the last of his beer.

Xander and a buddy had swept out the U-Haul and prepared to drop it off, and everyone else headed up to the third floor for pizza.

"Do you mind?"

"Not if you don't."

A heart-warming smirk greeted me. "I can handle all this." He waved around. "It's relatively sane in the grand scheme of things."

I laughed. "Then you really need to stay for lunch, because the crazy comes out when you dine at Dina's."

He stepped toward me, close enough for me to breath him.

A flicker of movement on my left caused me to turn my head. Randy was still outside and must've been hiding as I thought he went up to Dina's. I cleared my throat. Between him and my brother, Randy was the bulkier one; the kind of guy whose resting face is akin to Eastwood's – Go Ahead, Make My Day. Yet, he's the biggest pussycat around once you get to know him.

Korey backed up, putting a decent amount of space between us. However, it was too little, too late. Clearly, Korey caught the quizzical expression on my brother-in-law's face. "Shall we head up for lunch?"

"You go ahead, if you're okay with it. I just need a minute."

With a nod, Korey entered the back door of the building, and climbed up the stairs.

Explanations were in order as curiosity and an intense need to know flashed across Randy's face like a giant neon sign as he approached me carrying the empty case of Bud. "He's a nice guy."

"Korey?" I asked, but I knew better.

Randy was like an old soul, he was great at reading people.

Guess that's why he was a psychologist. "How come you haven't told anyone, or at least told me about him?"

I shouldn't have been surprised to hear a trace amount of hurt in his voice, but I was. "How'd–"

"It's obvious, at least to me and maybe a bit to Sean. He was watching too."

"Well it's not obvious to me. We're not dating. I'm not sure what we are yet."

Randy gave me that look, you know, the one that says you're full of shit, and you usually get it from a parent? Yeah, that look. "Something's there."

I glanced up at the building and wondered if Korey knew we were discussing him. "Maybe. Maybe not."

"Maybe? I see the way he looks at you, and the way you look at him."

"We're work friends."

"So? What difference does that make?"

"If we become partners and break up, it could ruin our work relationship. You said as much. And Ben confirmed as much."

Randy scratched his cheek and neck. "And you believe everything I tell you? That's a first."

"Because it was true." I hung my head a little.

"What about you and your live-each-day-as-it-comes attitude? Why are you so pessimistic about breaking up with this guy when you haven't dated him, or so you say, even though the attraction is clearly there? Dina and Xander have less chemistry." Randy put his hand on my shoulder. "Besides, he's definitely not Ben."

Ben Steinwald. My high school boyfriend until the night of my nineteenth birthday party and my cousin's wedding. Only one person knew what happened that night, and Randy was it. Sworn to secrecy and silence, he was the one who loaned me money to pay my rent that month because of what Ben did. I'll love him forever for both scaring the shit out of Ben and for keeping me together in the weeks that followed.

"If I were you, I'd make the most of it. You're young. Live wildly. Live like there's no tomorrow. Be bold. Be daring."

That's all I wanted too. "Be broke as well." I laughed. "I'm still trying to pay that off, remember?"

"Someday you'll be as old as me, and you'll have too many responsibilities to go out and party 'til the sun comes up."

"Too many responsibilities? Now who's sounding pessimistic? You're thirty. Your life isn't over."

"One might say, life is just beginning." He winked.

I cocked my head and stared at him, trying to read between the lines.

His blue eyes held a little mystery and interest.

"Wait… are you saying?" No way. It finally happened?

He nodded. "But don't say anything. Sean wants to wait until Easter to announce it. Doesn't want to take away from Dina and Xander's big official day of becoming one unit. But I had to tell someone. And I know you'll keep it a secret."

Easter was a week away. I could keep my mouth shut for eight days. I hoped. "Tell me now, all the details." Well, I had to know precisely *what* I was keeping a secret, right? Although I had a strong, sneaking suspicion.

"Well, the agency called and there's a baby coming for us."

I jumped up and hugged him. "Ohmygod, when?"

"Shhh," he said, glancing toward the building. "End of April."

"Oh god, when Dina hears…"

"The lists will start flying." He mimed writing note after note and tossed each over his shoulder. Oddly enough, it resembled Dina's mannerisms. "But she could be helpful in getting everything organized, even though I'm not fully ready for her level of involvement yet."

"Yeah, I don't blame you. Best to keep the lid on that for a while." My face split in half and stayed frozen in a perma-grin. I was beyond thrilled for Sean and Randy. A baby. They were going to be dads, after many long months of waiting. How fricken exciting. I wrapped my arms around him and squeezed him tight. "I'm so happy for you both."

"Thanks."

"Do you know if it's a boy or girl?"

He took another long pull of his beer. "No idea. We're meeting with the mom-to-be at the agency on Monday and we'll get the rest of the details."

"It's an open adoption?" Would the mom become part of their lives? Would they have to make a room for her in their house?

"Sort of. We're meeting her, but from what we understand beyond the birth she wants no further contact."

"Well, hot damn," I said. "This is the best news ever."

Randy gently shook his head with a zip-it look, and his eyes jumped to focus on someone behind me.

Korey walked towards us. "What's the best news ever?"

Panicked, I bit my lip.

Randy, always good at covering me, piped up. "Sean and I are thinking about getting a new place. Closer to Shayne. We never get to see her enough." He wrapped his arm around my shoulder.

"Oh stop," I said, smiling.

"Well, you are working, like all the time."

"I have Monday and Tuesday evenings free, and Saturday and Sunday days off."

Randy patted me firmly on my back. "And yet here you are helping out your big sister."

"Just like you, it's what our family does." My family had always been like that – ready to help out whenever help was needed. It was endearing, and a little hard to take sometimes, because there were times when you just needed to do things on your own.

Korey smiled at me, the corners of his eyes pushing up.

"And speaking of family. Your sister is having the most contained freak out over the bathroom. I've never witnessed anything so hilariously bizarre."

"Maybe I should go home." I laughed in jest and tugged my keys free from my pocket. I knew for sure the toilet paper rolling under and not over would be one thing that would piss her off. It's not like I tried to upset her, but it was kinda fun. Maybe tying the bow incorrectly on the guest towel probably wasn't the smartest thing either. But damn, the girl needed to relax about the little things. It was just a bow.

"Oh, this I got to see, and record." Randy patted me on the shoulder as he waved his phone. "See you upstairs?"

"Yeah," I said, reluctantly, and tucked my keys away. "I'll come face the music shortly."

"Everything okay?" Korey asked as soon as the door to the building closed.

"Couldn't be better." I wore the biggest, goofiest smile. Probably looked like an idiot, but I didn't care. Sean and Randy were going to be dads, my sister had moved back into the same city as me, and the man I wasn't sure about relationship-wise stood before me, having survived time in my crazy world. Yeah, I was over the moon.

"Shall we?" He extended his hand, palm up towards me.

With gusto, I grabbed his hand and squeezed tight, and led him back upstairs to face my insane sister.

Chapter Six

After pizza and more beers, we broke away from my family and changed back into our tacky polo uniform. Work lagged on and on with all the innuendo we said to each other, while trying not to draw attention to ourselves. Our cash out envelopes in our pockets, we raced over to his apartment. It was closer, and we were desperate to remove our clothes and rub each other raw.

"Your family is lovably whacked." Korey twisted a strand of my hair around his index finger and breathed deeply after our heated display of affection.

The clock blinked its time, announcing it was fresh into Sunday. But only by a few minutes.

"That's your bedroom talk?" I ran a finger down his masculine, perfectly chiseled chest, stopping just at that delicious dark line running from his naval to the golden goods south. "Figured you chat me up about my body, or the way I make you sing, or the wild and crazy things we could attempt together, but no, you had to bring my family into the bedroom." I laughed… a little. Happy as I was for a little break to catch my breath and slow my heartbeat, this was not quite what I had in mind.

"I just think you're very lucky. As crazy as your sister is, and she's certifiable don't get me wrong, she loves you. Same with Randy."

"Actually, Sean's my brother, Randy's his spouse."

"Right. You seem very close with Randy though." He shifted underneath me, so I could see his face.

"We are. He's been like a big brother to me for a long time. He and Sean were high school buds. Neither wanted to admit to the other that they were gay but when they caught the other dating someone else, they finally admitted their feelings. The rest as they say was history. They've been married two years now and together for four or five."

"That's cool."

"It was a shock to Mom and Dad, although both claimed it didn't bother them—the homosexuality part—it sort of did. But after a while, a long while truthfully, they accepted it, and Randy really became part of our family. However, it pissed off Sean that they so easily accepted Xander. Mom says it was because Sean broke them with having a serious partner, but I think there's more to it than that. Several times, I thought they were closet homophobes, but watching how they interacted with Randy, it wasn't true. I'd like to think they brought Sean up believing he'd marry a woman and produce grandchildren, so the falling in love with a man threw them for a loop. At least that's my take on it." No one wanted to ever think their parents were less than ideal, right?

"Think they'd be accepting of me?"

I turned to face him fully.

There must've been indecision clouding my features because he said, "Is it the way I look? A lot of people are turned off by the whole dreads look."

"It's not that. They were fine with you today."

"So, you're admitting it's you?"

I sighed and breathed a few times before speaking. My words needed to match the thoughts in my head. Too many times I've been accused of having verbal diarrhea. "I'm admitting the issue of my telling everyone I'm in a relationship lays with me because I don't know that we are." Or that's what I wanted. "There's no problem with the way you look. I think it's sexy as hell." I touched his dreads to prove it.

He tipped my chin with his left hand, forcing my face back up in his direction. "What are you afraid of? And you can't use the whole if we break up thing."

"You wouldn't understand." My gaze fell to his chest as it rose and fell with each breath.

"Try me."

Trailing my focus back up to his warm eyes, I flipped the question around. "What about your family?"

"What about them?"

"Would they be accepting of me?" I knew it was a dumb question, but I wanted to deflect from the elephant in the room. My parents would likely accept anyone who treated me with a modicum of decency. They were too blind to the things I kept well hidden. As far as I knew, they were in the dark about Ben and assumed we'd split because of schooling. If only…

"You're too straight and narrow." He laughed.

Straight and narrow? "Hey, I have hips and curves."

"God, you're cute." His fingers ran through my hair and he slipped his hand lower and grabbed my ass. "What I mean is you're, dare I say, vanilla? No tattoos, no weird hair, no unusual piercings. You're a straight arrow."

"They wouldn't like me because of that?" That was discrimination. Almost. My heart skittered, and my stomach flipped.

"Who wouldn't like you? Everyone likes you." He kissed the top of my forehead. "I'm just messing with you."

"That's mean."

Long fingers trailed down my back, the hairs standing up on end in anticipation. He drew a circle as he spoke. "My dad's a straight shooter. Works for a bank. Totally normal guy. Your dad and mine would get along really well."

Dads were softer when it came to their sons and their respective girlfriends. Moms on the other hand… "And your mom? Would she approve of someone like me dating her son?"

"So now we're dating?" His eyebrow stretched high into the retail space his forehead had occupied.

I choked on my own words. They did roll out a tad too easy. "I don't know. Can you call a weekend of hot monkey sex and moving my sister dating?"

He wiggled in bed, inching himself so we were eye to eye, and his manliness pressed against the inside of my thigh. "Hot monkey sex, eh?"

I started laughing, but when his lips covered mine, the laughter died. Our rest break was over, and bedroom talk flew out the window. Another round or two of animalistic, heart pounding, body glistening sex lay before us.

# # #

In the morning, I rolled over and reached for my glasses. It was nearly noon, and I had a few text messages from my sister. Nothing urgent, just curiosity about Korey. Actually, it was more like digging for gold so I turned off the screen, preferring to ignore her rather than deal with her.

Korey wrapped his hand around my waist and pulled my naked body close.

"You know it's almost lunch time." I tried wiggling out of his grasp, but he held tight.

"Are you hungry?"

Of course, and that's when my stomach growled, loud enough for him to hear. "Very much so. That chocolate and whipped cream at three am, while delicious, really did nothing to nourish me."

"Fine," he said, but he had a ginormous smile. "I'll make you something to eat." He rose out of bed and stretched. Buck naked, he walked to the door.

"Hey," I said, shielding my eyes and turning my head away. The internal heat from seeing his rump in all its daylight glory seared my cheeks.

"What?" He turned around, his nakedness dangling without an ounce of shame.

"Aren't you going to put some clothes on?"

"No. It's my apartment." He wore shock so cutely and gave me a once over.

I'd pulled the blanket up over my breasts and tucked it around my hips.

"Does it bother you? You saw me naked last night. All night. We slept naked. Hell, we were talking naked just now."

"Yeah but…" I didn't know how to explain it. We were in the bedroom, and it was night time, with nothing more than moonlight streaming in through the window. It wasn't the boldness of daylight, where nothing was hidden. Not that he needed to hide. His body was perfect. Distracting but perfect. I could lick his abs again, and his inner thigh.

"Hey." He cleared his throat, waving his hands to catch my attention. "I'm up here."

"You really need to put clothes on, I can't think straight when you parade around like that."

"Like what, this?" He slowly sauntered across the room, one hand on his hip, the other waving through the air. "This is parading."

"Oh stop." I laughed.

His strut was epically funny, and I fell onto my side as he twirled on the spot.

He pounced onto the bed and quickly straddled me. His fingers found the sensitive spot on my waist and he started to tickle me.

Laughter and peels of giggles poured out of me as he inched his hands and buried them into my flesh. "Stop," I breathed out. The tickling ceased, and I opened my eyes.

He hovered above me, the sweetest look of adoration on his face. "Come on, I'll make you breakfast, or lunch, as it is."

I pulled the thin sheet back up over my boobs. Apparently in my giggle fit it slipped down and exposed me. "Can I wear one of your shirts?"

He shook his head, and a sly smile crossed his face. "It's sexy Sunday. Stay in your beautiful nakedness for lunch." He pouted, this sexy, core warming pout. His hands were poised, ready to dig in and tickle some more. "Please?"

"Fine," I said hesitantly, still wrapped in my blanket. I worried I'd never be able to say no to this man when he looked at me like that. *Do I let the blanket fall before or after he leaves?* I tucked it around me a little tighter as my heart picked up its pace.

Korey rolled off the bed, and I admired the rear view again as he left. This would be a long meal, if we managed to eat much. Staring at him in all his naked glory was a huge turn on as the man was a freaking god… In the bedroom where it was just us. It was a little weird to be in the buff outside that sanctuary.

Dishes rattled from the kitchen, and I took the time to really check out his space and gather up my own courage to walk in the nude. It was dark when we arrived from Dina's, aside from the candles he lit once we'd gotten in and before we peeled the clothes from each other's bodies.

As I glanced around the bedroom, it really was very plain. The mattress was on the floor, atop a box spring, blankets, pillows and clothing scattered everywhere. The night stand beside me was a square box with fabric draping over it. I peeked under the green flannel, surprised to see it was a crate on its side but more surprised to see it filled with books. Books about anxiety and depression. The spines mentioned dealing with abandonment, and how to get over rejection. I felt supremely guilty for spying and dropped the drape back into place.

As shame filled me, I smacked my head with my palm. I'd reached a new low, resorting to snooping.

The rest of his bedroom was unexciting. A pale pink sheet covered his window, which made me laugh because he clearly had no shame about walking around in the buff and I highly doubted he was afraid neighbours would peek in. I looked out the window. It faced the back of a strip mall, a rundown alley separating us. It would be hard to stare up from the ground and get a clear look into the apartment.

A few of his clothes hung in the closet, but there was a pile in the bottom, and a shirt hung over the folds of the closet door. But no pictures. Nothing to give it a homey appearance. Hotel rooms had more decorations.

Sighing, I stood and stretched, my nipples firming up with the cool air now that they were no longer covered. I took a deep breath and swallowed down my fear at being so boldly exposed. It wasn't that big a deal. He did it and he was right, we had seen plenty of the other in all our naked glory yesterday, last night and early this morning. Sauntering down the hall into the kitchen shouldn't rack me with such anxiety. But the daylight hid nothinge. There'd be nothing to hide. And sunlight wasn't as flattering as candlelight or moonlight. What if I wasn't as sexy now?

But first, the ladies room beckoned. After doing my business and washing up, I debated using his toothbrush. His tongue had been *everywhere* last night, and it didn't bother me, so using his toothbrush shouldn't be gross, right?

I stared at the toothbrush and it dared me to take it and put it in my mouth. But I couldn't do it. We were in such a fresh relationship, it'd just be weird, too weird. Instead, I took a swipe of toothpaste, smeared it across my finger and hastily ran it over my teeth. I felt like I was a walking contradiction and it was a little off putting. Sure, I could have mind-blowing sex with a guy for hours and not be modest at all with my body, but to walk around naked? Weird. And the toothbrush thing? That was bizarre too, but it shouldn't be.

I shook out my hands and tipped my head back and forth like I was preparing to give a huge speech in front of the whole school. It's just Korey. Only one person. And he's seen every inch of me. Why was I so scared?

Trembling, I opened the door all the way and the scent of cinnamon tickled my nose. I followed it to the kitchen, covering my breasts instinctively as he came into sight.

"Don't." He stepped closer to me, the heat rolling off his sexy, sculpted body, and he gently reached for my hand, a fingertip grazing the top of my boob. "Don't be shy."

"This is very…" I didn't want to say weird, even if it was a little. I really felt out of place.

"Sit."

I could do that, and it would make me more comfortable as I could hide myself a bit more strategically if I sat at the far end of the table and crossed my legs.

"I didn't make anything fancy, just toast and eggs."

Oh my god, he made eggs on a hot stove naked? I imagined the burns he could've suffered and immediately my eyes went *there*. His manly parts hung lower than the top of the stove, but still. What about a splash of oil? As he turned, my face burned hotter than the sun.

He dropped a plate in front of me. "I didn't know how you like your eggs. Scrambled okay?"

"Yeah." I lifted the top piece of toast. "Is that cinnamon?"

"Never had cinnamon toast?" He seemed surprised and cocked his head back.

"Not since I was a child." It was an odd combo, but whatever. It was hot, it was food, and I was starving.

We dined in quiet. Not an awkward quiet, but a soothing one, which was odd. The whole morning was proving to be unlike anything I'd experienced before.

As I munched on my toast, keeping one arm strategically placed to shield my breasts from wandering eyes, I took in his space, curious. Again, the walls were bare. Just the basic white paint apartment buildings put up. His living room had a couch, a nice looking one – dark soft-looking fabric, and a matching oversized chair. A small tv rested against the wall and a Nintendo 64 splayed out on the floor, cords in a tangled mess. A huge black lampshade covered a beige base on an end table and it completed the ensemble. It was minimalistic at it's finest.

But the lack of pictures bothered me. No family photos. No photos with friends. Nothing.

I had pictures all over my apartment. In fact, I had a wall dedicated to random photos. Every couple of weeks I printed off a new picture and added it. It was my feature wall. Eclectic, but it defined my home as mine.

Korey's apartment was as stark as it comes. Barely furnished. I almost wondered if it was a rouse and somewhere else in the city he maintained a fully furnished swanky place, and this one he used only for his bed mates.

It was a sobering thought, and my eyes flickered between my empty plate and the cereal bowl of apples set in the middle of the table. Was that a lost packet of condom tucked in between the fruit? What a totally random place to store them.

I glanced over to his dishes. His fork and knife placed eloquently side by side, the way I've read in magazines as the proper way to signal that you were finished. I copied him and did the same.

"How was that?" He kept his eyes locked on mine, never wavering lower like I found mine doing.

"Delicious, thank you."

He rose slowly from his chair, his ass the target of my staring, and dropped our dishes into the sink.

I stood, and immediately knew why he stood slowly. The skin on my bottom ripped off and stuck to the vinyl seat, the heat and warmth from my ass having glued it to the seat. I was now terrified my ass would be all red and kept my back turned to the table, which wasn't any better than my girlie parts flashing in his direction. "Can I help you clean up?"

"Nope. It's all good."

It was hard to lean against the table and maintain some modesty. So I swallowed my awkwardness and uncovered my shame by bracing my hands on the edge of the table and letting it all hang out. Not that there was anything to hang out. My boobs were perky, and my tummy was as flat as I could make it, but still.

I was overexposed and trying to deal with it.

He dropped the dishes into the sink. "You're so beautiful when you relax."

"Oh, I'm not relaxed, but I'm trying." I let go and straightened up.

He wiped his hands on a dishtowel and strutted toward me. *It* moved left and right, back and forth. I was mesmerized and couldn't stop watching. My boobs didn't sway like that, did they? He cupped my chin, tipping my gaze up to where it should've been to begin with. "I'd like to take you out on a proper date."

"We work tonight."

"Tomorrow?" Tenderly, he slipped his hand around my waist and stopped at the small of my back.

"I have Jordan until three," I whispered as raw sexual heat built up in me when he pulled me closer. This amount of coverage I was completely cool with especially since we were chest to chest.

"Can I join you?" His mouth hovered near mine, begging to be licked and sucked…

I wrinkled up my nose. "I'd probably say no. When I have Jordan, I don't have strangers over."

He spoke softly, the sound of his voice stoking every single ember within my body, "We're hardly strangers."

Fire raged between my legs as an intense longing and thrumming beat to its own thunderous passion filled song. "Not to me," I said breathlessly. "But you are to him. And I don't invite people over to his house."

He pressed himself into my hips, his own need getting stronger and firmer. His fingers trailed down over my neck, slipping off my shoulders and down the length of my arms. My fingers clasped into his. "What about after?" His voice tickled my earlobes as he placed a soft kiss under my ear.

My body trembled with anticipation, and heat pooled between my legs; they were slicked up and begged to be touched. I shifted a little, parting them, extending an invitation to put out the fire. "I'll be available after three-thirty." I didn't want to discuss children. I didn't want to talk. What I wanted was for this burning sensation to roar to life.

"Great." His warm kisses dotted along my collarbone as he lifted me on to the table. His hands reached behind me and the sound of tearing foil filled my ears.

I braced my feet against the chairs and welcomed him back into my body.

Chapter Seven

A date. A real, bonafide date with Korey. Not just a sweet, sweat-inducing workout kind of date, but a true date. I wondered the whole ride home what this would mean to him, verses what it meant to me. Not so much about what it would lead to, because I really hoped it ended with chocolate and whipped cream again, but how he would perceive the date? Does this mean we're getting into a boyfriend/girlfriend status? Or was it still a casual thing for him? Was it still a casual thing for me? The feelings he's brought out of hiding weren't scaring me as much as I thought they should. Or would. Did that mean I was finally letting go of Ben, and learning to trust again?

Korey's so different, and I really needed to stop worrying. Nothing he's done, or said, or even hinted at, should make me believe I was just a play toy for him. Although I didn't mind. It was nice to have such an animal for playtime.

And our time together was fresh – so fresh. We'd only been intimate with each other for a weekend. A sex-filled weekend. Moving into a committed relationship still hovered on the horizon. Tonight was a date. Not a contract-binding agreement of girlfriend status. I could still do this. I could continue to keep him at arm's length, as I felt he was doing with me. I still wasn't sure if I was ready to let him into my heart as fast, and as much, as I'd let him into my body.

I raced home and changed into a dress. Nothing fancy,

just something I'd wear out casually. At the last moment, I grabbed a sweater to pair with it. Having no idea if we were going to be outside or not, I wanted the warmth. It was technically spring, but there were still remnants of winter frosting the grass and the temperatures nose-dived when the sun tucked its head into the horizon.

Korey buzzed at precisely three-thirty and I answered the door in a frenzy, excitement and eagerness leaping out of me at seeing him.

My mind screamed to my body to slow the hell down.

He stood, dressed in chinos and a blue and white plaid shirt, nice and different from our standard work uniform, looking smoking hot as always. His hair was pulled back into a ponytail, the dreads hanging every which way. The scruff of the beard neat and tidy, and the scent? Heavenly. It was crisp and fresh, a toss up between Old Spice and Calvin Klein. I only knew of the CK brand because Sean was such a loyalist, he only wore CK.

"These are for you." He produced a beautiful bouquet of mixed flowers. Lilies and carnations and daisies and an orchid splayed out between leafy greens and baby's breath.

"They're gorgeous."

"Not half as gorgeous as you."

The heat spiraled over my cheeks.

He pushed the flowers towards me, and I ushered him in.

"You're too sweet." It was the only thing I could think to say. Where did my brain go?

I rifled through my cupboards, sure a vase was hidden in there somewhere, but I couldn't find it. Instead I grabbed a pitcher and filled it with fresh water. I untied the bow securing the flowers and wrapped it around the make-shift vase. The flowers were sweet smelling, almost as sweet as the man who brought them.

Gazing into his eyes, I asked, "So, what's the plan for tonight?"

"I guess you'll see." He held his hand out.

"Let me grab my purse," I said, wandering around the wall

that separated my tiny galley kitchen from my even tinier living room.

Korey followed me and stopped when he saw my photo wall. "How…"

"Weird?"

"No, cool." His eyes never left the photos, taking them all in. "Who's this?" He touched a photo of a baby in my arms.

"That's my cousin's newborn, Samantha. I was there for her birth."

His mouth fell open. "What? Really?"

"Yeah. It was pretty much the coolest thing I've witnessed." Pride filled me. "I told her I was coming to play cards with her, as she was on bedrest. She told me that if she wasn't in the room, she could be in labour and delivery getting a stress test done. Lo and behold, she was in L&D when I arrived, and they took me in. Her whole face lit up and I found out she was in labour, so I tried to leave. But she wouldn't have any part of it. Fifty minutes later, Samantha was born." It had been a mind-blowing kind of day. Never would I have entertained the thought of witnessing a birth. And reflecting back, it had been the most beautiful thing I'd ever seen.

"When was that?"

"Samantha will be two next month."

"Wow." He continued to stare at the pictures. "So, is that how you got into being a nanny?"

I laughed. "No, I was never Samantha's caregiver. My cousin, Delilah, is a stay at home mom, but on occasion, we'll meet for playdates when I have Jordan."

"This him?"

He pointed to one of my favourite pictures. I'd been trying to take selfies of Jordan and I all morning without luck. Then just before the countdown ended, he turned his sweet little face up to me, the biggest smile spreading from cheek to cheek, and the camera snapped the pic. There's nothing but pure love between us. "Yeah."

"He's cute."

"And he knows it. Those long eyelashes? They get him out of a lot of trouble."

Korey hunched over and kept looking at the pictures. "Is it cool that I recognize some of these people?" He tapped some. "Your sister, your brother and brother-in-law."

"Yeah, a lot of family."

He stood but his focus remained on the wall, eyes searching left and right. "You're pretty close to them?"

"I suppose. We bicker lots, but we always make a point of getting together. Like next weekend. Mom has this elaborate spread every Easter, and everyone comes. My grandparents, my siblings. Sometimes a stray friend who's without a family to go to." I looked him in the eye when he glanced in my direction. "What are you doing for Easter? Going to your mom and dad's?"

He turned away, ignoring my question. "Where's this?" His short, nail bitten finger touched a newly added photo, but I wasn't interested in explaining.

"You didn't answer my question."

"No, I won't be celebrating Easter with my dad."

That's twice now he's mentioned a dad but never a mom. I felt that there was a reason, but I didn't know how to inquire about it. "Does he live here?"

"BC interior."

Ah, the interior of British Columbia. A majestic mountainous area with lush valleys. Not the answer I expected, but I didn't know why. "For some reason, I thought you grew up here."

He laughed, easing away any tension I thought was hanging around. "I've lived everywhere, but this has been the biggest city I've ever lived in." He listed places I'd never heard of. "I've only been here ten months. Moved last June."

"And lived through one of the coldest winters on record," I added.

"It wasn't so bad."

A puzzling thought came to my head. Is that why his apartment was so barren, because he moved around a lot? I swallowed down a morsel of fear. Of fear that if I started something wonderful with this man, he'd up and leave. See, I knew there was a reason I shouldn't get involved. My mind had gathered subtle clues that I'd failed to put together.

"What's wrong?"

I tried to hide my feelings behind a mask, but I failed. Clearly it was written all over my face. "Nothing."

"Oh, geez. When a woman says that, I get nervous, because it's usually something."

"What? There's no reason for you to be nervous." It's me who's nervous. "Honestly." I headed to the front closet and located my phone. "Let me take a selfie of us." For the wall. For the memories.

"How should we pose, and where?" He pulled me tight into his arms, kissing my neck.

"How about a sweet pose first?"

"Can do."

I stretched out my arm and framed us in the picture. Mousy me, with my boring brown hair and glasses a total contrast to his manly dreads and scruffy jawline. A reverse Beauty and the Beast.

He wrapped his arms around my waist and smiled. Seeing the glow on his face, it was hard not to replicate it and I smiled just as wide. I snapped a couple. It was easier to choose from a few than to only have one, especially if it wasn't great.

"Now a fun one?" I suggested.

"Ooh, yes." He spun me around. "Of us kissing."

I closed my eyes and leaned in, clicking multiple times just to be sure.

"Let's see."

Thumb on the photos, I flipped through. The happiness on our faces was perfect.

"This one." He tapped, and it became a favourite. "Send

this to me."

I did as instructed, sending the kissing one and the cute couple-like one for good measure.

"One more? A sexy one?" He pulled out his own phone from his back pocket.

I wiggled my eyebrows at him. "Later? And not on your phone. On mine."

He purred. "Meow." And planted a kiss on the tip of my nose.

With the knuckle of my finger, I pushed my glasses up. "Thought we were going out?"

A gentle kiss graced the top of my hand. "Yes, let's." As I closed the door, he asked, "Do you like spicy food?"

"How spicy are we talking?"

"Freeze your toilet paper for later spicy?"

I laughed, so much for sexy-times later. Hot food didn't love me the way I loved it. "Is that an official label for spiciness?"

"You bet your ass it is."

He drove me to this place on the south side of the city that served the best *laal maans*, at least according to Korey. The exterior was a run-down strip mall until you stepped through the doors. When the outside doors closed behind you, huge wooden doors lay ahead, and beyond that, you moved into another space and time. The over-powering scent of spice took my breath away, in a good way. Suddenly, it made me ravenous.

The décor was rich and full of colourful tapestries, acting as dividers between tables, at least that's what I assumed, as I never saw anyone else. Our area had a small table, and a pair of the largest floor cushions I'd ever seen. It was dark and yet flickering streams of candlelight danced across the heavy fabrics, illuminating the golden threads woven within. I truly felt as if we'd been transported across the globe.

The music had to have come from hidden speakers,

because I didn't see the musicians. It was delightful, very east-Indian and easy to get into the rhythm of the beating drums, even if I couldn't tell you the difference between a sitar and a tabla. When I closed my eyes and truly listened to the beats and melodies, it filled my soul on a sexy, yet spiritual level.

Once seated on the giant, velvety floor cushion, a beautiful server, dressed in what I could only describe as a belly dancer's outfit, moved the fabric wall and entered our private little space. Silently, she passed us two menus, speaking only when inquiring about drinks.

I ordered a Diet Coke and got a strange look from Korey.

"You don't order a pop here. Are you allergic to anything?"

I shook a no, and he ordered two drinks that I probably couldn't even spell if given half a chance, let alone pronounce.

It was warm in our little space, and as I shrugged out of my sweater, the thin straps of my dress fell over my shoulder.

Korey leaned closer and deftly, with his finger, slipped it back up, the electricity coursing through my arm with his lingering touch. "Later, remember?" he whispered, and a pool of warmth flooded over me. In the glow of the candle-light, he looked even more handsome, yet rugged and earthly, as the flicker of shadows danced over his face.

Our server appeared and set down two steaming, dark-coloured drinks and a plate containing strips of bread and dip. Without a word, she bowed and backed out.

He ripped the bread and dipped it into the white sauce and held it beneath my nose. "May I?"

I closed my eyes, inhaling the scent of fresh bread and a rich aroma of garlic? I didn't know as I grew up in a very western fed culture where pasta and pizza were normal, and never, ever did we dare taste anything exotic. The bread touched my tongue, and a cascade of tastes surrounded me; flavours I'd never experienced but suddenly was in love with and hungry for more. I bit off a chunk and slowly, delicately chewed while opening my eyes.

"Good, eh?"

I couldn't speak.

"I figured I'd start you off with something easy. That was a garlic dip."

And it was freaking fantastic.

"Have a drink." He nodded towards the glass mugs.

The liquid, which resembled coffee, was anything but. It was sweet and intoxicating, and it burned all the way down where it set my insides on fire with its spicy flavour.

Between the bread and drink, and the music and the low lights, I just knew this was going to be a magical evening, and I did everything I could to savour the moment. The moments, actually. The seductive tease of him feeding me bread was just the start. Our meal lasted for what seemed like hours, but it was the between courses that really set me on fire.

Maybe it was the way the music, with its sensual and rhythmic beats, coursed their way into my soul. Maybe it was the way the food, all spicy and new, warmed me up from the pit of my stomach to the tips of my fingers. Maybe it was the drink, and something inside allowed me to shed my inhibitions. Whatever it was, it was sexy and seductive, and I fell hard under its spell.

When he pulled my cushion close and slipped a piece of bread into my mouth, his other hand roamed my body, trailing a tingling path to another area where heat and wetness were the new norm. His fingers danced and dipped inside of me to the beat of the music, while I instinctively opened to him. It was the riskiest thing I'd ever done in a public setting, but I felt uninhibited. And once the sweat rolled down my heated face, I returned the risk, feeling his desire as I rubbed my hand across the bulge in his shorts.

I may have felt we were all alone, but he always seemed to notice when the tapestry would move and cover either himself or me, acting like my euphoric expression was completely normal. The server paid us no attention, simply placing new food or drinks on the table. Perhaps this was expected? I had no idea, but it was the best damn meal I'd ever had. When our time at the restaurant concluded, and we were full physically and emotionally, Korey paid our bill and we raced back to my apartment. Our physical bodies needed to connect and lock together the way I felt our souls touched over that ethereal meal.

Chapter Eight

After that rousing Monday night escapade, the rest of the week paled in comparison. I just needed a full night's sleep, and as hard as it was, I went home alone after work, but not without a heated kissing display beside my car.

Friday night rolled around, and I looked forward to sleeping in on Saturday, which I did. At Korey's apartment. Sunday morning was a different story. We both woke up in my apartment, early. No time for sleeping in. It was Easter Sunday and we were expected at my parent's place by eleven, with desserts and appetizers.

I parked in front of their house and looked over at Korey. He was the epitome of calm—relaxed shoulders, and a broad smile on his face. I wonder how he did it. My own calmness had flown out the window as soon as I left my parking stall. This was the first celebration—ever—I was bringing a guy to. Yeah, he helped move my sister, but he was my friend back then. Now, he was my boyfriend. Someone I felt very connected to and was starting to develop feelings for. So much for keeping everything on the down low. It scared me.

"Are you ready?" I asked, waiting to see if there'd be a crack in his façade. Nope, nothing.

"I should be asking you that."

I pulled down my visor and touched up my lipstick. "I'll be fine." A quick glance out the rear-view mirror as I watched a burgundy car pulled up behind me. My grandparents. "Can you carry the plates? I'm going to help Grandma."

He nodded, and I was out of the car, waiting beside Grandma's door.

"Shaney girl," she said, her voice cracking. "Grab the buns, will you?"

I held the grocery bag and offered her my free hand. Her weathered hand slid into mine, and with the grip of a forty-year-old she nearly broke my bones pulling on it. When I looked up, Korey stood beside my grandfather.

"Granddad, this is Korey," I said in a loud voice. Granddad was deaf in his right ear.

"Sorry?" His old, gravelly voice cracked.

"No, Korey. K-k-k."

"Ah," he said, smiling. But I knew he didn't quite hear. Normally he'd address the name properly.

Korey stood there, a couple of plate of homemade snacks in his hands. "Can I help you, sir?"

"Nah." Granddad closed the car door. "Ah, fiddlesticks. Would you grab my cane, Tory?"

Korey reached into the back seat and passed the cane over to my grandfather.

"Stay close," I whispered.

Grandma and I shuffled up the walk; Korey and Grandpa were steps behind. I twisted the handle and entered the house. It was what we did – the doors were always unlocked and the guests were always welcomed.

No one seemed bothered that Korey was with me. I don't know if I expected a repeat of the moving day where everyone stopped mid-conversation, but it never happened. Everyone milled about in the kitchen while Dad and Sean sat in the living room, flipping through the stations.

"Make yourself at home," I said. "You know everyone."

"Hey, Korey, right?" Xander walked over and passed him a beer. Drinks were never in short supply in my family.

"Thanks, man." With a quick twist, Korey removed the lid and took a swallow of Bud.

Randy caught me by the arm and spun me around. "Can you come help me with the gift in the truck?"

I looked around sure that everything was running smoothly, and Korey was holding his own. Didn't know why I worried. He fit right in. "Sure." He acted funny, nervous even as we excused ourselves and walked out to his SUV. I tugged on the end gate. It didn't budge. "You need to unlock it please."

He leaned against it.

Suddenly I worried for a different reason. "What's going on? Did everything go okay with the baby lady?"

Bracing himself on the edge of the bumper, he said with a smile, "Better than okay. She wants us to be there in the delivery room so we can witness our child being born and be the first to hold the baby."

My eyes widened. What a great gift that would be for them, and they'd be able to share that story with their son or daughter. "Did you find out what she's having?" I rested my butt against the end gate as there was no point in trying to open it. He hadn't unlocked it yet.

"No. The birth mother didn't want to know, figured it would be a great surprise for us."

"So you'll get to be…"

"The first to see." He wrung his hands together as his chin lowered. "But Sean doesn't want to be in the room when it happens. He's more comfortable pacing in the hall."

"Yeah, I can see that. He's squeamish with blood." When I was little, I fell and sliced open my calf on a piece of busted concrete from the foundation. I screamed for help. Sean was the first to find me and he nearly hurled when he saw the cut muscles and exposed bone. It was Dina who ended up carrying me back to the house and ringing a neighbour to take me to the hospital. Poor Sean. He felt so bad, but seeing blood and all that, it weakened him. I understood what Randy meant. Birth wasn't a pretty event for most, it was bloody and messy.

"And I can't do it on my own." He hung his head and kicked at a rock. "So… I was wondering, would you join me? You were there for Delilah."

I blinked and moved my head in shock. It went from side to side to a strong up and down motion. "I… wow. Yes. Sure. I don't know how I can help though."

"When we talked with JodiLynn, we mentioned we had a sister just a bit older than she is, and she was excited. She doesn't have any sisters."

"Am I supposed to be friends with her?" I didn't want to be rude, but between the two jobs, the new boyfriend and now being asked to attend the birth, there wouldn't be extra time to befriend this JodiLynn.

"No. But she's young and scared."

My judgey brows climbed high. "How young?"

"She's fifteen."

"Fifteen? Fifteen?" I couldn't contain my shock. Fifteen was still a child. Barely in high school. She shouldn't be having a baby, she was practically a baby herself.

When Delilah gave birth, she was in her mid-twenties. Even at that age, the idea of giving birth terrified her. What would a fifteen-year-old think was happening? Suddenly, I wasn't sure I wanted to be in the delivery room, watching as a frightened child pushed something out of her body, an intensely private part of her body. If she screamed and yelled in terror, it could kibosh my desire for having kids someday, and I most definitely wanted them.

"She doesn't have anyone to lean on. She's in foster care, abandoned by her mother." Randy placed his hand on my shoulder, and sincerity crossed his face. "I know she's young, but she's healthy, and the baby's healthy too." Randy glanced down the street as a minivan full of people parked four houses away. "No one's willing to give someone like us a family. Except this lady. Just meet her and see."

Someone like us. The words hurt me, and they weren't even

directed at me.

Randy and Sean would make better parents than some of the ignorant, neglectful ones I'd spotted at playgroups. Just because they were gay didn't mean they can't raise a child.

It was ironic. There was this fifteen-year-old who probably got pregnant the first time she had sex, and there was my brother-in-law, who'd been waiting all his adult life to become a dad but was denied because he wasn't in a heterosexual relationship, yet the child-mother procreated at the drop of a hat. It was bullshit and monumentally unfair. They'd make such great parents, doting and loving on their child. I just knew it.

I looked over Randy's shoulder towards the house. The next major-major gathering, not like the get togethers we usually had, would be Thanksgiving, and he'd be bringing his son or daughter to this. This baby would change everything, but only for the better. Nodding my head, I agreed to meet the birth mother. "When?"

Randy's face split in half with a smile and his shoulders dropped. "Thank you." He wrapped me in a bear hug. "We meet with her at the agency on Tuesday afternoon."

"Great," I said. "Send me the information. I could have Jordan with me if it's early afternoon though."

"I don't have a problem with that, in fact, it may even help."

"I'll see what I can do." I made a mental list to plan my day, so that depending on the appointment time, I could either get Jordan down for a nap, or have him up and ready to go. Playgroup may be the key to wearing him out. For now, I needed to focus on the original reason he brought me out here. "What did you need my help with again?"

Randy opened the end gate and passed me a box. "Take this," he said, grabbing a tray of goodies. "And I'll carry the sweet stuff."

"What's in the box?"

"You'll see." He winked.

I had a feeling it was something to do with the baby, but I was willing to wait and find out.

"Wait…" He closed the end gate. "How are things with Korey?"

I flipped my gaze back to the house. We were all alone. "Really good."

"You decided to take the plunge? Make the most of things?"

I swallowed. "I know it's so early in our relationship, but I think I'm having real feelings for him."

"Like the butterflies?"

"No, well yes, definitely that, but it's more than that. I feel so connected to him, like we're two sides of the same coin." An image of the sweet man floated in my brain, and slowly he did a dreamy strip tease, tossing each article of clothing. "I feel as if…" I sighed. "Like maybe he is different than Ben."

"That's a good thing."

"Yeah, it is." I pushed the saran wrap tightly around the bottom of the plate as it had lifted a bit. "But I was so blindsided by him. We'd been together for thirteen months." There'd been conversations, foolish ones in hindsight, about moving in together before we started college.

Randy cleared his throat. "I don't think Korey is like that."

"I hope not." But I wasn't sure. As much fun as we were having, I wasn't sure if I could open up to him about what had gone down. How would he react? Heading back toward the house, I stumbled on the lip of the sidewalk and almost dropped the box.

"You okay?"

The plate waivered in my hands but thankfully never left. "That was close." I smiled and paid more attention to where I was walking.

"Korey treating you like a lady should be treated?"

Flashes of tangled limbs and sweaty skin filled my mind. When I looked at Randy he was shaking his head. Was it clear what

I was thinking of?

"You know what, don't expand on that. I'm just happy that you're happy."

"I'm very happy."

"Good." Randy opened the door, and we walked inside.

I set down Randy's gift and gave a nod towards my big brother, who was still engaged in conversation with Dad. I assumed Sean knew that I knew about the baby, given that he gave me a friendly wink and looked lovingly at Randy.

I walked over and wrapped my arm through Korey's and listened to Dina and him bicker over the colour of beige paint, which I found odd because I'd seen Korey's place and its total lack of colour. Maybe he was trying to rattle Dina which was really easy to do. I tuned most of the deeper parts of it out, but I got a kick out of how he kept egging her on. It was subtle, and she kept missing it. Even Xander, who joined in a few minutes after me, seemed to notice as he turned his head and laughed a little.

I loved my sister a lot, even though she was a little thick, but I suppose that nitpickiness would suit her well with her interior design business. She planned on going into business on her own, running it from her apartment until she could afford to own her own store. I had no doubt in my mind she'd be wicked at it. When Dina set her mind to something, it always worked out for the best. I envied my siblings for that kind of drive. Apparently, I missed out on that gene, as I still struggled with the whole 'what to do with the rest of my life' part.

And a decision was needed. The meeting with my advisor about my career path was quickly approaching.

It was nice having Korey at the dinner, and I couldn't remember what I was so worried about to begin with. Korey blended in so seamlessly; it was like he'd always been there. He laughed with the family jokes and produced a few of his own zingers. At meal time, he dug in and complimented mom on the food. I could tell by the eyebrow waves my mom gave me, that he was scoring a few points in her books.

Is this what falling in like was? Finding that perfect person you didn't know had been missing until you see it altogether and wondered how you ever did without? Because I wasn't sure how I managed without him in my life before.

"Before we all clean up for dessert, can I give you a gift?" Sean looked at my parents.

Randy produced the ample sized box and set it before my parents. It was big enough to fit a microwave in but was much lighter.

"What's this for?" Mom asked, tugging on the bow.

"Just open it, will you?"

She nudged my dad. "C'mon, Harry. Help me."

The bow went flying and my dad tore at the purple wrapping paper. Mom opened the box and pulled out another wrapped box. It was like a Russian nesting doll. Each box only slightly smaller than the previous one. Finally, after five boxes hit the floor and coloured paper covered the hardwood floors, they unwrapped the last one—a picture frame.

"Is this?" My mom stared at the orange and black photo and showed it off to my dad.

Sean nodded. "Sure is. You all know that Rog and I have applied to adoption agencies and reached out to surrogates in our quest to have a family."

I beamed and gave Korey's knee a squeeze. Joy was radiating out of me and I couldn't keep my hands off him, nor the stupid smile I felt had been plastered on my face. However, it paled in comparison to the pure excitement coming off Sean and Randy as their baby's profile face my confused parents.

"Someone who has answered our prayers. Her name is JodiLynn, and she's due in three weeks, and that's our baby."

Cheers erupted from all around the table, and hugs were plenty.

"Hot damn, we're going to be grandparents." My dad tapped Granddad on the shoulder. "You hear that, Pops, I'm going to be a granddaddy." He gripped the picture frame. "That's my grandbaby."

"What you say?" He fiddled with his earpiece and a grumpy growl lingered on his face.

"Old man doesn't hear anything." He dismissed his dad's comment with a wave.

"Three weeks? Oh my," my mom said, her eyes lighting up with the news. "That doesn't give us much time to get you boys all set up. You'll need a crib and a dresser and–"

Sean and Randy stared at each other. "Mom, we're practically all set up and ready to go. We'll just need to pick up baby clothes, but we don't know yet what colour we'll need."

Randy leaned his head on Sean's shoulder. "The day after we found out, we went shopping."

"Bought out West Coast Kids," Sean added.

"Can we throw you a baby shower at least?" Mom asked, searching around the table but her focus went straight back to the framed photo.

"Yes, a baby shower. We can make it a gender reveal theme." Dina jumped into full planning mode. "We can have pink and blue balloons tucked into a box, or a cake that's either pink or blue and when you cut into it–"

Sean put his hand on Dina's shoulder, silencing her immediately. "Let's slow down, Dee. There's a ten-day period after the baby's born where the mother can change her mind. So, until that point, we'd rather not. But on the eleventh day, absolutely, let's go into full celebrations. But we'll already know the sex."

"The eleventh day it will be," Dina said. "I'm so happy for you." She hugged her brother again.

"I'm thrilled too." Sean's smile had yet to fade. "We're going to be dads!" He fist-punched the air.

Suddenly I couldn't wait to meet with the girl who had brought so much joy into my brother's life and meet Randy and Sean's son or daughter.

Chapter Nine

"I'm sorry I'm late." I raced past the hostess stand while wrapping the apron around my waist. I was thankful I had the foresight to hang my uniform in the car and change into black pants as Aimee came home a smidge early. Never thought I'd be changing into my top at the stoplight three blocks from work. I figured I'd have at least a few minutes before my shift started.

Speed walking into the staff change area, I pulled out a lock and secured my things into a locker before sprinting back to the front of the store.

Niall hadn't moved from his position at the cash register. "I'm going to have to write you up for this, Jade."

Shit. I'd hoped not, but what could I do? I was twenty minutes late and my phone battery didn't have enough power to send an outgoing call before it died. I hung my head. "I'm sorry."

Niall pointed to the far corner of the dining room. "You have a table at B8." He gave me a quick glance over. "Straighten your name tag, please."

I re-adjusted the pin, correcting its diagonal direction into one perfectly horizontal. With a pad of paper in my pocket, I walked over to my table.

Jasper was across the floor, working the best section tonight. How lucky for him. I didn't even get the second best. Joy was holding that area down. Instead, I got the worst section, which on a normal Thursday evening, if I was lucky, I may end up serving twenty tables all night long. If the weather stayed decent. Unlikely with the dark clouds rolling in.

Order scribbled on the notepad, I punched in their order, my fingers jamming on the touch screen with a little too much force as the screen rainbowed around the edges.

Jasper snuck up behind me. "Hey, pretty lady."

"Hey." I spun away from the computer and marched into the server station.

Jasper caught up with me. "What's with the cold shoulder?"

I looked over at Niall, who still stood by the till, flipping papers and writing on the backs. His normally chipper façade was gone, replaced by a perpetual growl. In a low voice I whispered, "I'm late."

Jasper stepped closer as he paled. "As in…"

"Not showing up for work on time."

He visibly relaxed. "Oh. That."

"What? You thought I was late, like, as in with my period?" For real? On my god. As if. I was on the pill and took it like clockwork and he used a condom. Every. Single. Time. There was absolutely no way we'd even. But wow. I couldn't believe that was the first thing that came to mind. "No, I was at the agency with the lawyers, meeting with JodiLynn. But thanks, you know, for jumping straight to that conclusion."

Glasses slammed on my tray with enough force to rock the ice inside.

Jasper poured a couple mugs of coffee and walked away, huffing as he went.

Watching him storm off, I reminded myself that this was why dating a co-worker was a bad idea.

"Hey, you're here," Joy sang out as she grabbed herself a tray. "I hope everything is okay?"

"It is, and I apologize for being late." I filled the glasses with cola.

"It's all good. It happens. Being late. Sorry though, as Niall gave me the L's."

The L's – a section littered with booths. Perfect for couples and families. And the preferred place for most of the guests. My section for the night was tables, where the groups sat. It was also the section most likely to getting slammed when it got busy and the booths were all full.

"But if you get overwhelmed, just ask and I'll help you out." She touched my arm. Always so sweet, I really enjoyed working with her. There was something about her that calmed me and after she let go of my arm, I didn't feel as angry anymore.

# # #

The supper rush ended as fast as it started. Damn storms.

I was clearing off a vacated table, likely my last of the evening, when Jasper approached me. "Sorry for earlier. For thinking that."

"Why would that be the first thing that sprang into your mind?"

He shuffled his feet. "There was this girl I dated, and she used that line on me. Twice." He held up two fingers for good measure.

"Well, I'm not her."

"I know. Sorry. It was a gut reaction."

"You didn't even notice I wasn't here?" I crossed my arms over my chest. For sure I would've missed seeing his face if he was absent. He was kind of hard to miss.

He gazed into my eyes. "I did, but I figured you were in the back." A soft caress slid up my arm as he ran his hand over it. "Let's not fight, okay?"

"Okay." My resolve softened with his touch.

"How'd it go today?"

"It went well. Sean and Randy and their lawyer met me at the agency. I never knew there were so many people involved in an adoption before. Figured it was pretty straightforward."

Jasper nudged me over to the bussing station, away from customer's prying ears. "Really?"

"There was a social worker, someone from the foster home JodiLynn's staying at, Sean and Randy, their attorney, and I think she was a lawyer in training as she represented JodiLynn." I counted them all off on my fingers. It had been a roomful and trying to keep everyone straight was hard.

"What's she like, the birth mother?"

"Scared. She sat beside me the whole time and kept looking at me."

"You were the one closest to her age, I'd think."

"I was. Everyone else was much older. Except for the training lawyer. She was younger." Like closer to Randy's age, if even that old. "But JodiLynn's young, and very pregnant." I mimed how far out her stomach stretched. "She's been under the care of an OB for the past four months and everything is going well. She's attends regular school and plans on being a doctor. Now that she's picked the parents, she keeps in touch about her doctor's appointments and all that."

"Does she seem like she'd become attached to the baby?"

I shrugged. "I didn't get that vibe. Sean's lawyer asked how involved she wanted to be after the birth and she shuddered. She wants nothing to do with the baby and wants to go back to living her life." Whatever life it was that allowed a fifteen-year-old to have sex and get pregnant. But she was in foster care and I was more than a little curious as to why her mother would abandon her. Oh well.

The last table in Joy's section left, leaving the restaurant devoid of customers. Just staff remained, and it was only eight.

It was quiet, the rolling thunder beyond the walls, and the gentle beats of country music overhead.

"I love this song," Jasper said. "Do you know it?"

I cocked my ear toward the ceiling and listened. It wasn't familiar.

"How can you live in Alberta and not know Paul Brandt?"

"Because I don't listen to country music."

"So, you probably don't know how to two-step either?"

"Ah, no." Hanging out at the country bars wasn't a pastime of mine. Hanging out at any bar, really. I much preferred the quiet to the racket and pounding.

Jasper extended his arms. "Let me teach you."

"What? Here?" Yes, the dining room was empty but that wasn't a valid excuse to dance around it.

"Why not? We're allowed to have fun while we work." He placed a hand on my waist and held my right hand. It felt wrong. And weird.

I pulled back.

"Joy, do you know how to two-step?"

"Of course," she sang and moved into position with Jasper. A couple of head nods and they were off, two-stepping through the dining room. Joy's laughter filled the space, and they developed quite a nice rhythm, moving as a solid unit through the B section and up into the R's. At the end of the song, Joy curtsied to Jasper. "Thank you."

The volume of the music turned up a notch and Niall walked out to the front. "I love it when the staff enjoy themselves."

Another country song started.

Niall extended his hand to Joy. "May I?" And the two were off.

"Really?"

Jasper grinned. "It's not the first time this has happened." He stood so sweetly with his arms opened wide. "C'mon. It's not that hard. You can't be worse that that." We both followed Niall and Joy as she led them around the dining room.

I hoped I was better than that and begrudgingly slipped my hand into Jasper's. "Let's give it a whirl." It had to be quite the scene as I fumbled around, stepping on Jasper's toes once, and bending with a little too much enthusiasm that we nearly bonked heads. Eventually, Jasper gave up and wrapped me in his arms.

"Just do a box step," his voice a low whisper in my ear. "You can box step, right?"

A slow nod came his way and I managed to make less of a fool of myself than Niall had.

"You've got it," he said, and immediately threw me off my rhythm as he swept me off my feet and spun me around.

Delighted, I tipped my head back and laughed. Caught in the moment, I went to kiss him, but he quickly deposited me on my feet and cleared his throat.

"Customers."

Niall waltzed up and greeted the couple. "Care to join our little party?" He grabbed two menus and led them over to a booth tucked into the centre, giving them a little bit of privacy. "Joy will be with you in a minute." He walked over to the cash register and put his finger over his lips. "Not a word to anyone. Meghan especially."

I didn't know who Meghan was, but I suspected she'd be upset to have seen that. I zipped my lips, as did Jasper and Joy.

Our fun on a temporary hold, I went into the server station and wiped down the counters.

Jasper whispered in my ear, "We can finish what we started later. My place tonight?"

A blush crept across my face and I pushed up my glasses. "Sure."

Chapter Ten

I met my best friend Lily for a much-needed drink. It had been a helluva ten days although it felt like weeks had passed.

Slipping into the booth, I flagged my server down and ordered myself a draft. I desperately needed a cold one, nice and foamy.

Lily marched into the restaurant, huffing and puffing, her skin flushed right into her hairline. She tossed her phone on the table. It skidded across stopping beside the candle.

"One night! I choose to go out one night and he can't be alone with the girls for five minutes before he's calling and asking what he should be doing. I swear, babysitters are more deductive in figuring that out. Good lord." She threw her purse onto her seat and slumped into the booth.

The server set down my beer with a curious expression upon her face and greeted Lily. "Can I get you anything?"

"Yeah," she said, eyeing my drink. "I want one of those."

"But you don't drink," I said, stating a fact. Lily was usually the designated driver when she was lucky enough to go out with friends. Must've had a bad day.

"Well, if I have one, Jason will need to wait an hour before I'll be even able to come home and rescue him." She ran her fingers through her dark hair, fluffing it out over her shoulders. "Never get married, and never, ever have babies." She closed her eyes and cracked her neck.

"I'm sorry you're having a rough night."

She sighed and scanned the restaurant. "It's not your fault."

"Anything I can do? Do you want me to babysit one night so you and Jason can go out together? Maybe you need to go out with each other, and not separately."

"I don't know. Maybe." She propped her head up and softly closed her eyes for a breath. "I'm just bitching. I'm sure in a few years I'll look back on these days and laugh."

I raised my eyebrow at her.

"A girl can hope."

"Well, I hope that things get better for you."

Swiping back her curtain of hair, a small smile formed at the edges of her thin lips, outlined to look more plump and full. It failed, and I'd subtly tried to tell her. "Whatever. I live vicariously through you anyways since my life is over. So, dish… What's going on in your world?"

"So much. I'm not sure where to begin."

Lily waved her hand in a rolling movement. "Start with the most boring. Work. I'm sure it'll only get more exciting from there."

The server set down Lily's draft and took our orders.

"Oh, can I get a straw?" Lily asked.

"A straw? Sure." The server nodded and took off.

"What for?" I asked, mirroring the servers contained curiosity.

"I hate the taste of beer, and a straw will have it bypass my taste buds and just give me the buzz I'm looking for."

I gave her the weirdest look and shook my head.

"Stop worrying about something as unimportant as a straw. Tell me. How's Westside?" She waved her hands frantically. "I keep meaning to pop in there and have you serve me."

I glanced around the restaurant. It was much busier than we typically were on a Tuesday night, which is why only two servers worked those nights. I let the cold, bitterness of the beer drown out my worries. "It's good. Nothing much has changed there. I get along with everybody." Even Evanora, although she's harder to please than everyone else.

"Ooh, *with* everybody?" She placed way too much emphasis on *with.*

I hated that I blushed so easily.

Korey's name hadn't even surfaced and here I was turning shades of red just thinking about the place we worked in, the places we visited. The way he danced and made me feel like I was the only care in the world. The way the candlelight caressed the golden sheen of his pecs on the nights we worked out until the wee hours of the morning.

"So how is your god?"

I needed a sip to cool me down. Hell, I needed the chug the whole mug, but that wasn't going to happen. "He's fabulous."

"Tell me…" She stretched out her neck, eager to take in every word I said.

"He's wonderful." There I said it and stopped hiding the smile thinking of him always brought out of me. Each day was better than the one previous. I wasn't sure if my budding feelings were the result of hours of glorious love-making, or if it was something more. The idea of falling in love… But it was too soon. And I wasn't ready. I had plans, and a boyfriend wasn't a part of them. I sighed, a soft, dreamy sigh. "Unlike anything I've experienced before. He takes me to new heights."

"That's the sex talking." She dismissed my comment with a wave.

"It's not, but that's so…" What was the word I wanted? "Orgasmic. The places we've been."

She lowered her voice before glancing around. "What? Where?"

"Well there's this one restaurant."

"Oh stop, you did not." She shook her head.

"I kid you not and it was the best non-sex we've ever had.

It was individual and personal, and risky and hot. So smoking hot." I fanned myself for effect, just remembering the enclosed space. The smells. The beat. "I sat on my cushion and his handiwork. Oh my…" The heat radiated off me. I'm sure the condensation forming on my beer was a direct result.

Her eyes rolled as the server dropped off a straw. "Ah, to be young again."

"You and Jason should check it out."

She laughed and stuck the straw into the beer, taking a long sip. "It'll never happen."

"Not if you don't go."

A third of her beer disappeared in a heartbeat, and she pushed the mug to the side. "Honey, there's too much of me in the way. The only way he gets access anymore is if I roll on my back and point an arrow at my vag and scream it's open. And even then. It never happens. The kids wear me out and I'd rather roll over and try to catch a few zzzs, not get all messy with sex."

I gave her a sad smile. "You really should check that place out. Even if nothing happens, just take in the music with the belly dancers, and the food. That was the best East Indian food I've ever had."

"That shit's spicy. I can't even imagine what it would do to my insides."

I looked at Lily. The mom sitting across from me clearly needed a night out, away from her kids, away from her responsibilities. She needed to be lit up, needed to remember what love was all about. Surely her and Jason had been horn-dogs at one point in their relationship. Not all relationships turned so sour, did they?

"Well, I'm glad you and Korey are getting along so well. Enjoy it while it lasts because as soon as you say I do, you don't." A sad smirk rolled over her face and her shoulders slumped inward.

Instantly I felt bad for her.

"How's that affecting work?"

"It doesn't." I was really surprised by that. We had that one small fight, if you could even call it that, but otherwise, we kept it mostly professional. Mostly.

I shared with her how he's very much in his Jasper character when we're at work, and I was very much Jade. I was the newbie he still taught - like how to handle a full tray of drinks - and yes, my wrist and forearm are getting much stronger. But in quieter times, he kept me on my toes and he taught me how to two-step throughout the dining room. We have fun at work, but absolutely no kissing or love tapping or anything that could be construed as PDA. Aside from that one time.

With any luck, it seemed we're passing on that enthusiasm on to our customers because the tips have been great. I'd finally paid off my credit card, and the debt load on my line of credit was shrinking, and the pocket for my college fund was building. I felt guilty about keeping ten percent of my cheques as fun money, but it was nice having spending money once again. A couple more months of hard work and I should be completely debt-free, or damn close.

"Did I tell you, Aimee is pregnant?"

Lily scoffed. "Really? Moving on to two kids, is she?"

"Yeah, she's fresh. Not due until November, and I know she'll be going on mat leave at some point, so my time with Jordan will change." My heart ached just thinking about how little time I had left. The next six months would fly by. The past few months certainly did.

"Yeah but not for a while." Her phone lit up and before she answered, she slurped back the rest of her beer and produced a satisfied look on her face. "Hah, now I'll need to wait a bit before I can drive home. Hello?"

I tried not to listen to her tone and the condescending voice she used. Surely Jason couldn't be that inept with his own children? I think Korey could figure out how to bathe a toddler. Well, one maybe. Jason did have three children at home, and Tuesdays were bath night. At least they were with Lily, as she'd mentioned that to me before.

"Where were we?" she asked, tossing her phone to the side. "Don't get me wrong. As often as I'd like to wring his neck, I can't imagine my life without him. I just wish he'd figure some things out on his own."

"I'm sorry." I wasn't apologizing for Jason's behaviour, just acknowledging that parenthood was tough and sometimes you just need a friendly shoulder to cry on. Or bitch to, as was my case.

"Anyway, you were saying… about the job?" Our food arrived, and Lily ordered another beer before she tore into her burger with great zest. "Oh my. Hot food. Food I don't have to cut into a million little pieces and serve up." She took a man-sized bite. "Oh, this tastes so good."

"They really do make the best burgers." I cut my burger with a fork and knife, and placed a forkful in my mouth. It was sinful how good it tasted. The jalapeno wasn't overpowering, but just enough to give it the perfect zing. "I'm meeting again with JodiLynn tomorrow."

Her mouth was full of food, but it didn't stop her from saying, "Remind me who she is?"

"The birth mother."

"Right, for your gay brother." She tore off another bite and mumbled out a thanks to the server who put the beer on the table. Lily transferred the straw and took a long sip, shaking her head after.

I hated that phrase - 'my gay brother'. If he wasn't, would she have addressed him as my straight brother? It maddened me why that needed to be thrown in. But this wasn't the time to get my panties in a twist, as Sean would say. He'd also tell me there are bigger battles to fight. Channeling his words, I took a breath and refocused. "JodiLynn's young, and it's really hard to overlook that. I feel terrible for being so judgey, but she's a child."

"Fourteen?"

"Fifteen, but just." I picked at my burger, shoving the lopsided tomato back in as I cut off another bite. "But she's okay with me being there in the delivery room. In fact, I think she was a little relieved that there'd be another female in the room."

"Was she raped?"

"She never said, and I never asked." And the thought never really crossed my mind until now. As I dwelled on it, it just made the whole situation worse. It was traumatizing enough to be raped, but to carry the rapist's baby? A whole new form of torture. Suddenly, I felt bad for JodiLynn and the circumstances possibly surrounding the baby's conception. In my mind, it was better to think she'd been knocked up by a boyfriend. It was stomach clenching to think it could be more vicious than that.

"When she due?"

"Next week sometime."

Lily pounded back the rest of her beer. "You've cleared this with your work? Labour is unpredictable. Look at me." She chomped on a fry, bits of it falling out of her mouth. "Maggi came two weeks early, and labour lasted for days." The word days drawled out for a few seconds. "Myrah was two weeks late, but a pretty fast labour. And Mary? She was ten days late and we barely made it to the hospital. Almost gave birth in the back seat of the Tempo." The French fry in her hand wagged in my direction. "You never know with labour. I'd make sure your boss knows."

"Oh, he does, and he's pretty cool about it. Korey's pretty excited about it too. He came with me to the library and we took out all these birthing books and videos, which he watched with me."

"Lucky you," she said smugly. "I could barely get Jason into prenatal classes. I'm glad Korey's working on that interest with you. Hold on to that boy." She smiled, but it wasn't a warm, genuine one. Instead it reeked of ugliness and bitterness. "Are you excited about helping her out?"

"I think I'm more excited for Sean and Randy. They've been waiting so long, and I just know they're going to be the best parents, and in a small way, I can help them with that. If I can keep her calm, then maybe the birth won't be so traumatic for her."

Our server stopped by and cleared away our plates.

"I'd like another draft please," Lily ordered.

I was shocked and stared at my best friend. "Really?"

"Yeah, is that okay with you?"

The snarky tone rattled me. It was unexpected and was very unlike her. Still, I wasn't her mother, or Jason, so I nodded.

"I'll be right back." The server walked away.

My phone pinged with an incoming message. *Korey.*

Are you coming over tonight?

I typed back without hesitation. *Out with a friend but maybe after?*

I'll be waiting.

I tucked my phone away as I could feel a glare rolling in my direction. It's not like I was the only one who texted during supper. She'd answered a call from her significant other.

Our server was fast and approached our table quickly with another round for Lily.

"Thanks." Lily transferred her straw and started sucking back the pale liquid.

I couldn't do anything aside from watch in a mix of rapt fascination and horror. it was crazy how fast the beer disappeared up the straw. It was almost like she wasn't even breathing. I swear, the glass was empty in less than a minute. "Good lord, Lily."

"I know, right?" She tried to conceal a burp but couldn't lower the volume on it. She brushed it off. "I didn't think I was that thirsty. My burger must've been extra salty."

"I don't think it's thirst." I leaned over the edge of the table. "Are you okay?"

"Of course. Don't you sometimes just need to let loose?"

"Yes, but…" Thirty minutes ago I was encouraging her do that very thing, and now that she was, I shouldn't be nagging her, right? But this was so unexpected. Watching her pound back the beers made me lose my focus. I couldn't think about anything more than worry about my friend and getting her home. There was no way she'd be fit to drive, especially since she never drank and had three within a very short time. I could handle that, and I'm sure I'd be fine to drive but not Lily.

As I sat back in stunned silence and contemplated what my options were, Lily covered her face. When her hands fell, tears streamed down her face.

"Lily, what's wrong? What's bugging you?"

"Everything." She buried her head in her hands. "I want to leave him."

My heart plopped into my stomach. I gave her hand a squeeze. How does one deal with that? "Have you talked to Jason about that?"

"When would I? By time we get the girls into bed, he's asleep because you know, he's the one making the money and should be bright eyed and bushy tailed for the morning." The venom fell off her tongue and her eyes rolled.

"Did he say that?"

She glared at me, her eyes narrowing into thin slits. "It's what he's thinking."

"Oh, Lily. You really need to talk to him about how you're feeling. Maybe talk to a therapist."

"Yeah, cuz we can afford that."

A flyer that hung in the staff bathroom flashed in my head. "I'm sure there are programs, or something. Talk to you family doctor, or the girl's pediatrician. Someone."

"I am. I'm talking to my best friend."

"And I'm honoured you're sharing with me. But I can't help you the way a professional can." I reached my hands out to hers.

With a violent shove, she pushed them away. "I don't need help. I just need someone to listen to me." She slid out of the booth. "I'm going to the bathroom."

When she was out of sight, I texted Korey. *Going to be a while. My friend is drunk and I need to take her home.*

Where are you?

Oil City Burgers.

Don't leave until I get there.

Okay. I stared at my phone as if it had all the answers. By staying silent, it proved it had none. I flipped through my social media channels and glanced towards the restrooms. I was just about to go and check on her when she came stumbling back.

Her colour was gone, replaced by an unhealthy shade of grey.

"I got sick."

"Yes, you did." Suddenly that vile smell hung in the air and surrounded us. I stood and flagged down our server. "I'm sorry, I need the bill right away."

She took one look at Lily and rushed off, returning a minute later with the bill and a card reader.

"I got this," Lily said and pulled out her wallet.

She didn't look up at the server, who whispered, "She's not driving home, is she?"

"No, I'll be taking her home."

The server patted me on the shoulder. "Good."

The bill paid, I helped Lily out of the booth. "Give me your keys."

Lily fumbled through her purse and dug them out, passing them over. "If you're going to drive me home, how will you get home?"

"Don't worry about it."

She leaned against me, and I turned my head away. Her breath reeked with bitterness and was making my stomach roll. Not a good feeling. We were at the door when a breath of fresh air greeted us.

Korey, my knight in camo shorts and army green tee, sauntered up the sidewalk.

Chapter Eleven

"Hey," I said, my face splitting in half with the biggest smile. It never got old seeing him. The butterflies swirled; my heart pounded a little faster and my breathing came a little quicker. "What are you doing here?"

"I told you I was coming."

The text message flashed in my brain. "Right." I'd completely forgotten in Lily's drunken mess.

"Who's this?" Lily slurred.

"Lily, this is Korey."

I couldn't tell what look she gave him, but I saw his reaction and the subsequent blush. "So, *this* is Korey. Your very own knight in shining armour." We lumbered down the sidewalk to her minivan.

Korey went on the other side of Lily and shouldered her while I opened the door.

"He smells nice," she said, running her hand down the side of his face before Korey pulled away.

Very untypical behaviour for Lily. It made me cringe but not for any other reason than embarrassment. I felt bad for her.

She dropped her hand and braced herself against the van door. "Why are we taking mine?"

"Because if you get sick, I don't want it in mine."

"I don't want it in mine either." Her face morphed into fear.

"So don't get sick." I opened the back of the van, hoping to find a plastic bag or something. Surely in the mess, there had to be something. Success! I found a baggie, it wasn't big, but it would do the job if she felt the need to re-empty her stomach. I passed it to her and rolled down the window before I closed the door.

"Where does she live?" Korey asked, closing the distance between us.

"Heaney Landing."

"Where's that?"

"About ten minutes away." I was still confused by his actions.

"I'll follow you." He tilted his head and answered the utter blankness on me face. "So, I can bring you back to get your car?"

Face-palm to the forehead. "Oh right." Too many things going on to keep everything straight. I hoped he didn't think I was a complete idiot.

He leaned down and gave me a kiss, short and sweet.

Nope, guess I wasn't that much of a dumb-dumb.

"Get a room," Lily said, anger in her voice.

I climbed into the van and started it up.

"I get it, you're in loooovvve. You don't need to parade it to the world." She turned her head out the window.

Disgusted by the nasty tone of her voice, I put the van into gear and silently drove her home. It sucked to hear such venom coming out Lily's mouth, but I tried cutting her a little slack, knowing her home life was less than ideal and that she was drunk and unwell. But her words still stung.

I pulled into her driveway, and Korey pulled in beside me.

Together we escorted the staggering Lily up to the front door, after securing her van.

"Do I unlock the door? Or should I knock?" I whispered to Korey, searching through the keys to find the one that resembled a house key. They all did. *Shit.*

He shrugged but after a moment's hesitation, rapped his knuckles against the door.

A bewildered Jason opened the door, anger and then concern covering his face. "Jesus, Lily, what's wrong?"

"She had a few beers over supper and got sick."

He wrapped his arm around her. "Oh, honey, are you okay?" He wiped her sticky bangs away from her eyes and escorted her to the couch where he gently set her down and covered her with a throw blanket. As he'd been playing video games, he moved the controller on to the nearby table and flicked off the lights, sending it into semi-darkness.

I set her purse down on the bench by the door, dropping the keys beside it.

Jason sauntered over, constantly turning his head to check on his wife. "Thank you, Shayne, for bringing her home. I could've come and got her."

"Yeah, but then you would've had to wake the girls and all that, and I know she'll need her van tomorrow."

"Thanks, I appreciate that." He addressed Korey. "Hey, I'm sorry, where are my manners? I'm Jason."

"Korey."

"Were you out for dinner too?" A hint of a questioning eyebrow surfaced.

Korey stepped back and waved his hands. "No, no, no. I texted Shayne and she told me what was going on, so I came to help out."

"Mighty nice of you." Jason clapped him on the back. "Do you have a ride back?" he asked me.

"Yes, Korey followed us."

"Oh right," Jason said, covering his forehead with his hand and quickly turning in Lily's direction when a groan fell out of her. "I'd invite you to stay—"

"No, I get that she needs to get to bed." Korey opened the door for me, and we stepped onto the front porch. I hesitated. It wasn't my place to interfere, but I'd never seen Jason be anything less than a doting husband the couple of times I'd seen him. Behind closed doors, things could be different, but still.

Would I be her friend if I didn't say something? It was a hard place to be in. I swallowed and chose my words carefully. "You need to talk to her, Jason, like really talk to her. Not tonight, but soon. Okay?" I glanced over to my friend who had curled up on the couch and started snoring.

He looked in Lily's direction and turned back to me. "Yeah." His voice heavy with concern. "Thank you for being a good friend for her. I know she appreciates you."

Maybe. I nodded and bid him goodnight.

Korey stood beside the passenger door and opened it upon my approach. "I'll take you back."

I slumped into my seat and buckled up.

"Are you okay?" Korey gave my thigh a rub.

"I just want to go home." I leaned my head against the head rest and watched the lights blur as we drove past. I couldn't understand where the tears came from, but not wanting to attract attention by moving my hands to my face, I let them silently stream down my cheeks without wiping them away.

He parked beside my car and killed the engine. "Do you want to come back to my place, or did you want to go to your apartment?"

I shrugged, still not looking in his direction.

"Are you wanting to be alone? Although I don't think that's the best idea, if that's what you want, I'll comply. Or I can just hang out with you and not say a word and be a shoulder for you to cry on."

I faced him and took in the sincerity on his face. How in the world did I get so lucky? "I'd like the latter, if you don't mind?"

"Never." With a gentle caress from his thumbs, he wiped away the tears and planted a kiss on my forehead.

Thirty minutes later, I curled up on Korey's lap on my couch, the glow from a romantic comedy playing on the tv being our only light source.

Korey draped his arm over my right hip, making soothing circular motions. "Anything you want to talk about? You're unusually quiet."

"I'm just thinking." And it was the truth. My mind hadn't stopped tossing around thoughts since I'd watched the door close at Lily's house. I took my glasses off and gave my eyes a rub.

"About?"

"My future." I rolled and looked up into his face, keeping my head in his lap. "I wonder if I'll be like that. Miserable with where my life has gone."

"Is that what she is?"

"Oh yeah." Our fingers found each other and tangled together. "I knew she was unhappy, but we all have moments like that, right? But she's really miserable." I locked my gaze onto his. "And I'm really worried about her. She said she wants to leave him."

"Talk to her in the morning." A gentle snicker escaped him. "Or maybe mid-day, she might be hurting in the morning."

"I don't know." I rolled back to face the tv.

Too many thoughts and emotions. Was she really thinking about leaving Jason? Would she take the kids with her? How could she man-handle Korey like that, if she was so upset in her own relationship? Was I being immature to be mad at her for the way she talked to me about Korey and the way she groped him? The alcohol was to blame-in part-but she wasn't that drunk.

"Are you upset with her?"

"More than I want to admit."

"Because?"

A nice soothing feeling spread over my body as Korey stroked my hip. Up and down. Up and down. I let a soft sound out that was half a sigh and half a groan. "Her behaviour was unreal. She drinks her beer with a straw. She looked at you with disgust, like a bug that needed to be squashed."

"You got that from that look?" He sounded surprised.

"That, and the way she touched you."

"Yeah, that was weirdly uncomfortable."

"Aren't you mad at her?"

"Nope, and I'll tell you why. If you are and you decide like girls do, to stay mad at her and hold a grudge and I agree with you, when you get back together, suddenly I'm the asshole because I thought once she was a bitch. It doesn't matter that you had agreed with me on it, but that's what you'll remember. I called your best friend a bitch." He raised an eyebrow. "So, I'm going to remain neutral. I will listen and promise to remain objective."

"Is that what you think? She's a bitch?"

"See? I mention it in the what-if-realm and now you're asking." His hand moved up to my shoulders, and stroked down the length of my arms, capturing my fisted-up hand.

I stared up at him, wondering about what he went through with his former girlfriends to cause such a brick wall of insecurity. "Who was she?" I blurted out before I put my filter in.

"It doesn't matter," he said after a few heartbeats pounded. His expression remained mostly unchanged, but I noticed the twitch in his left eye.

"I'm sorry. For whatever she did."

"It's all good. That road led me to you." He brushed hair off my forehead.

"You're sweet."

"Tell me something I don't know." His tone was full of a joking nature, and he tipped his head back as he laughed.

There's something inherently sexy about a confident man. He needn't be cocky, but self-assured. Like Lily said, I really was a lucky girl to have found such a prince. I was about to tell him, when my phone vibrated deep within my pocket. I chose to ignore it, thinking it was probably Lily, and I wasn't in the mood to talk to her. However, it didn't stop.

Sighing, I pulled it out of my pocket. Sean's name lit up my screen. Panicked, I pushed the answer button.

"Shayne, it's time." Sean's voice pitched with excitement and emotion.

"Already?"

"Yeah, her water broke an hour ago. There's no contractions, but she's at the hospital. We're in room 6. In labour and delivery." If I didn't know better, I'd swear he was already pacing the halls, a pinched expression of worry on his face.

I sat up, my eyes locking with Korey. "Do you think I need to be there now?"

There was a long pause and some muffled voices on the other end of the line. "Nooo." He drew out the word nice and long, the edge of confusion on the tip of his tongue.

"Sean, are you okay?"

"Yeah." His voice cracked. "I'm just really excited. We both are."

My heart pounded with excitement. This was it. My brother was going to be a dad. The energy pulsed through me and I couldn't sit still any longer. "Well, let me pack up a quick bag and I'll head over. I'll text when I'm on my way."

"Thanks, Shayne." He ended the call before I could say goodbye.

"Baby time?"

"Soon." I shared with him the minimal details I had received. My body had taken on new life, and I paced around the living room trying to burn off the heightened feeling. "A bag..." With a hop in my step, I grabbed the duffle bag from the bottom of the closet and filled it with items I thought would be helpful in a labour—a squeezie ball, a spray water bottle for the mom in case she became hot, unscented lotion for back rubs, hair ties, and mints for me. No labouring woman wanted someone to talk to her with foul breath. I thanked the video for that tip.

"All packed?"

I looked around the living room, sure I was forgetting something. "I think so."

"Like that video said, you just being there is going to be comfort enough." Korey touched my shoulder, instantly soothing me even though I wasn't rattled.

A mental list floated through my head, items checked off one by one. "But what if I forget something?"

"I'm sure you won't. And the nurses will be there. They are trained to help. After all, that's their job."

"I know. Nurses are golden."

He grabbed my duffle bag and hoisted it over his shoulder. "Don't forget to breath and take care of yourself too." A long finger of his touched the tip of my nose. "Take breaks if need be."

I nodded. She wasn't in labour yet, so it could be a long night. Not wanting to forget my purse, I eyed it to remind myself.

Korey eclipsed my view and stood before me. "Call or text me with any updates."

"Okay." My hands started shaking as doubt filled me. What if I couldn't do this? What if I did or said something that screwed up the birth and made everything worse?

"Hey, it'll be fine."

"I'll just keep reminding myself I'm doing this for Randy and Sean. They're going to be dads."

"And you are going to be an aunt."

Wait, what? Why hadn't I thought that before? *I* am *going to be an aunt.* I was going to help my niece or nephew enter the world and meet his or her dads. A smile broke across my face. "I can't wait." I reached behind him and grabbed my purse.

He held my hand and brushed his lips across mine. Like a fan on the embers, the fire rose like a flash between us. Suddenly, I wanted rip our clothes off, make the kiss last forever and bask in the naked desire brewing. But I couldn't. Not now.

His hand slipped around the ass of my jeans and he squeezed a handful. "Later."

"I almost wonder if we have time now?" I knew I really shouldn't.

"Sometimes anticipation will heighten the pleasure for later." His eyebrows waved at me, and my insides pooled into mush. "You should go."

"You're a tease." But I grabbed my coat, trying to deny that I'd rather stay and finish this first.

"I know."

We stepped out into the hall after I locked my apartment and headed hand in hand to my car, thankful that Korey had shown up at the restaurant to follow us to Lily's house and back to mine. He really was a keeper, wasn't he?

"Text me details."

"Even if it's middle of the night?"

"Yep. I'll probably be up." He handed me the duffle bag and tenderly placed a kiss on my cheek.

I turned into it and leaned into him, sucking and nibbling on his bottom lip, the desire between us growing with each passing heartbeat.

Firmly but gently, he pushed on my shoulders. "You need to go."

"I know." I glanced down to his shorts. A little tent action was going on. "But I–"

"Later," he said with a smile. "When we can take our time."

With a sigh, I climbed into my car and blew him a kiss.

Chapter Twelve

The nurse spoke softly to JodiLynn, as we all found out that anything higher pitched than that caused her to curl up in a defensive position. "JodiLynn, I can see the head now. It's staying put."

This was the good news we'd been waiting for. She'd been pushing for what seemed like hours, although it was less than seventy minutes, with the head appearing and then retreating after each contraction ended. The nurse had explained once the head stopped moving back, the birth was much closer as the baby was closer to the entrance.

I stole a peek over to Randy, who surprised me when he said he needed to sit down. I thought he was the stronger one.

His colour was returning as slowly as this baby was making his or her debut. The first time he saw the top of the head, he nearly passed out.

Whispering in his direction, I said, "Are you going to update Sean?"

He pulled out his phone and fired off a text. Sean, who had said from the get-go that he was not going to watch the birth, had excused himself from the delivery room when the nurse declared JodiLynn ready to push. According to the brief updates, Sean was wearing a path out on the floor of the waiting room.

JodiLynn grabbed my hand, and I returned my focus to her. With my free hand, I ran the damp cloth across her forehead and reminded her to breathe. Her face was red and blotchy. She grunted and squeezed my hand impossibly hard and the bones smashed together.

"Okay, we're calling in the doctor," the nurse announced in a quiet voice. "You can call in your husband," she said to Randy.

"He's good until it's over." He pushed himself out of the chair and stood, leaning on the side of the bed.

The nurse kept her focus on JodiLynn's centre but continued to speak sweetly. "If you'd like, Randy, we can draw the curtain closed. Would be shameful for him to miss that first cry."

"Ask him," I said between my own laboured breaths. The strength from JodiLynn's squeezes hurt my hand and stole my breath.

Randy's thumbs typed fast. "He's on his way."

I beamed, glad that my brother would at least hear the momentous sound.

The doctor, who I'd met earlier this morning when he made his rounds but totally forgot his name, breezed on in. He kept his voice low. "Looks like we're about to meet the baby." His hands locked behind him.

I waited. Waited for him to glove up and check things out and poke around like doctors do, but he just stood there. Silently. Watching. A couple of contractions passed, and he moved closer to the foot of the bed. "How are you feeling, JodiLynn?"

She opened her eyes and glared at him. "I never want to have sex again." Her head hit the angled bed, but only for a moment. In a heartbeat, she curled like a cat and continued to squeeze the life out of my hand while grunting.

His voice calm, he said, "That's it. That's a big one." The nurse had ready blue latex gloves which he slipped over his hairy hands.

Finally.

I allowed my gaze to fall to her privates. Everything had changed so much over the last couple of pushes that it was hard to describe, but in between the purple flushed skin was the most beautiful head of hair I'd ever seen. It was dark and plentiful, and growing larger by the second.

I nudged Randy over and felt him standing beside me. "Look," I whispered.

"Jesus Christ," he said, surprise evident in the high-pitched voice. The colour that had returned fell out of him in a flash.

I glared at him.

"Sorry." He lowered his voice and cleared his throat. "JodiLynn, you are truly remarkable."

As she grunted some more, excitement took over me. "Oh my god, I can see eyebrows."

The doctor nodded at the nurse and stood closer. "JodiLynn, you'll feel my hands putting pressure under the baby's head as I catch your baby, okay?"

"Please… don't…. touch me," she cried out in broken sobs.

"I promise to try my best." He whispered some doctor speak to the nurse, who rubbed the labouring mother's leg. It all sounded foreign to me, but his voice wasn't agitated so I wasn't too worried.

"This is the worst part, JodiLynn. The intense burning you're feeling will pass in a moment."

Her scream echoed off the walls and froze in my heart. It was shattering, like being ripped in half, which I suppose the baby was truly doing, or at least it probably felt like it.

"I need you to pant like a dog, JodiLynn." The doctor's voice firmed up a little, but it was enough that she heard and, more importantly, followed.

I elbowed Randy. "Is Sean coming?"

The sweetest nose and lips emerged out of JodiLynn after she stopped screaming.

"I'm here," my brother said from behind the salmon-coloured curtain.

"Good thing," the doctor said as he suctioned out the

nose. "You're about to meet him or her."

Sean and Randy's baby wasn't even born yet and it was the cutest baby ever. That sweet flattened nose, those lush and full lips.

"Next contraction will push out the shoulders. You're almost done."

Big tears fell from her eyes. "I don't want to do this ever again."

The doctor whispered in a barely audible voice. "They all say that." He winked at me.

"You've got this," I said to the girl who was giving the gift of life to my brothers. "You are incredibly strong."

She hunched her shoulders to her drawn up knees, and I watched in amazement as the baby's shoulder emerged and the rest of the baby slithered out from JodiLynn. The most amazing sound filled the room; that of a crying newborn. As the legs were born, I saw the sex but zipped my lips. It wasn't my place, but I knew my brothers would be thrilled.

The nurse did the honours. "Congratulations, Randy and Sean. It's a girl."

I didn't need to see Sean, still hiding behind the curtain, to know he was crying. His voice cracked as he said, "Thank you, JodiLynn."

Huge tears fell from my face, and I wiped them away before I ran the cloth over the birth mother's face. I placed a tender kiss on her cheek. "Thank you for your incredible gift."

She finally released my hand and turned to face me, eyes bloodshot but devoid of any emotion. Beyond exhausted, she barely breathed out, "Thank you for being here."

Suddenly, she no longer looked young. Gone was the innocence of youth, replaced by wisdom most women my age had yet to experience. Her eyes became glassy, but she refused to make eye contact with the baby.

The air continued to be pierced with the most beautiful sound of a healthy newborn cry. I looked to Randy who was also crying, but he had the biggest smile to accompany it.

The doctor produced a pair of scissors. "Would you like to cut the cord, *Dad*?"

Weeping and sniffing, Randy stepped out from behind me to the foot of the bed. His hands shook as he severed the physical connection between mother and daughter.

The doctor passed the newborn over to the nurse, who placed her into the warmer. "You can come and watch."

"Sean?" Randy asked as he approached his husband. "Want to meet your daughter?" He poked his head around the curtain. "Just keep your back to everything."

Sean held Randy's hand and the pair of them slipped over to the baby warmer.

My brother's voice cracked. "Oh my god, she's beautiful. Thank you so much, JodiLynn."

Randy rubbed Sean's back and they tipped their heads together. "She's just as pretty as her mother." To the nurse he said, "Can I touch…"

"Of course you can."

Watching his face morph from bewilderment to pure love was astounding. Here were two people grateful to finally have the child they thought they'd never be blessed with. "Hi, baby girl. I'm your daddy."

I wiped away more tears as they declared their love and protectiveness over their daughter. It warmed my heart to see them so overjoyed.

"Okay, JodiLynn. One last push."

What? What did I miss? I looked down just in time to see a slimy, purple balloon fall into a metal tray. I'd forgotten a placenta still needed to come out.

The doctor turned it over in his hands. "It's all there." He set the tray aside. "Now, I know you're not going to like this part, but I need to check for any tears."

She whimpered and grabbed for my tender, and likely bruised, hand.

Behind me and to my right, the baby cried, her lungs expanding with each cry.

I swallowed down the biting pain as the bones mashed back together, but it wasn't as bad as hearing the muffled cries from my left. *Poor JodiLynn.* Her face was tight and yet, tears still slipped free. She winced and jumped as the doctor palpated inside her.

"Okay, I'm done," he said as he removed his hand. "Amazingly no tears. Well done."

She didn't acknowledge his comment and turned her head off to the side, away from me, the new dads and the crying baby she had inside her just minutes ago.

"Everything good with the baby?" The gloves came off and the doctor stood by the new dads.

"Apgar's of eight and nine."

"Perfect." He clapped Randy on the back. "Congrats." To JodiLynn, he said, "All the best with your schooling."

She still didn't acknowledge him, but she did release my hand. Finally.

The doctor shrugged and exited the room.

The nurse lifted the bundled baby. "Who would like to hold her first?"

"You go ahead," Sean said, "you were in here the whole time."

The nurse settled their daughter into Randy's waiting arms. "There you go."

Randy beamed while Sean snapped pictures, his teary eyes still focused on the bundle of joy he held on to with all his might.

The nurse came over and explained to JodiLynn what she needed to do but JodiLynn barely registered; her face blank and her eyes sealed shut.

"Is she okay?" I asked the nurse.

The blood pressure machine started whirring, and a low heartbeat filled the room. Her blood pressure and pulse were within normal. "She's likely exhausted." The nurse flittered around her, explaining step by step what she was doing, and within a few minutes, the birth mother was covered back up, no longer exposed to the world.

I wiped her face with a fresh cloth, and finger brushed her hair.

JodiLynn's eyes blinked and she stared into my mine. "Thank you."

"You okay?"

"I'm so tired."

"Would you like to see her?" Sean asked the exhausted birth mother, stepping closer to the bed.

"No, I'm good." She closed her eyes.

The nurse went over hospital policy with regards to keeping the newborn in the hospital for a period of twenty-four hours, and where the dads could spend the night with the baby as they couldn't stay with JodiLynn after she was moved to the post-partum area.

Overwhelmed by a lack of sleep as I glanced at the clock and noticed it was ten twenty-two in the morning, I knew I needed to go home.

Yawning and stretching, I said goodbye to the mother, and then to Sean and Randy.

"Do you want to hold her?" Randy asked.

I looked at Sean. "Not until after you both have." I patted Randy on the back. "I'll come by later."

Sean gave me a big hug, pinning my sore hand.

I winced.

"Thank you for everything."

"My pleasure." A yawn escaped me, and I covered up my mouth. "Sorry."

"Go home," Sean said.

"First, I need a new family picture." I snapped a picture of their beautiful daughter—my niece—and texted Korey. *It's a girl.*

Chapter Thirteen

I blinked several times to try and figure out where I was. Everything was dark. Like being in a room with the lights off. Like being wide awake and so drunk nothing made sense. It looked like Korey's apartment, but why?

I sat up and refocused after giving my eyes a rub with my left hand. "Korey?"

"Hey." He came into focus. "How was your nap?"

My eyes widened, and I studied him. "What time is it?"

"It's four-thirty."

"I got to go to work."

"No…" He walked over, holding a bowl of cereal. "You need to catch up on your sleep and get your hand examined."

"Why?" I should've looked before asking. My right hand was swollen, and a hideous purple shade coloured it. I attempted a fist and winced.

"That." He looked at my hand. "You babied it, and I figured it was sore, but I was starting to worry as I watched it swell."

"Shit."

"Did she break your hand?"

"I hope not." But I couldn't help but wonder. She did squeeze it hard and I felt bones rub together, but broken? Was that even possible? You'd have to be Thor strong to break a hand in labour. "Let's get it checked out." A yawn opened my mouth.

“Attractive,” Korey said in jest.

Foul unbrushed-in-nearly-twenty-four-hours breath wafted up my nose. “I need to brush my teeth.” I excused myself and cleaned up a little. The cool of the water felt nice on both my face and hand. My palm looked normal, at least as normal as I remembered, but the top of my hand was a dead giveaway that something was up, especially with the pain shooting through.

Since we were at the hospital’s walk-in clinic getting my hand checked out, I figured I’d pop by and say hi to the new dads. Korey was more than happy to tag along. I knocked gently on the door of the room the nurse said they were in. It was unusual for a baby to not be in the room with the mother, instead with the adoptive dads in separate room.

This room was tiny, with only one bed, and a solitary window that gazed right into the side of the hospital. I spotted the baby bed but should’ve known better than to assume she was in there. Instantly, I looked to Sean, who sat in a rocking chair, baby girl resting on his chest.

“Hey,” he whispered as he turned to us. It had only been a few hours but fatherhood suited him. He was all lit up and radiated joy. Day old fuzz covered his cheeks and chin, but he looked older, wiser. And most definitely happier.

“Congrats,” Korey said and shook the men’s hands.

Randy beamed like he’d won first place in contest. “Want to hold your niece yet?”

I thought he’d never ask. The biggest smile I had crossed my face. “Yeah,” I said.

Sean rose in one fluid motion, and placed the baby into my bad arm, the one with the bruised, but not broken, hand. Holding her tight, I touched her gently with my finger.

“What’s this?” Randy pointed at my bandages.

I *had* tried covering it with my long sleeve shirt. “It’s nothing.”

Randy hovered over me and his daughter, running his hands under my sore one. "Did she?"

"It's not a big deal. I swear." My eyes flitted around the room. The last thing I needed them to worry about was me. They had a precious bundle of joy to devote their energy to.

"Oh, Shayne." Sean's face contorted into his big brother concern.

"I swear, I'll be fine." I brushed off their expressions. "How's she been?"

That did it. The crack in the Grand Canyon was nothing compared to the split on their faces. I've never seen them so overjoyed.

"Awesome," Sean said.

"Fantastic," Randy said at the same time as they gazed at each other. A new love blossomed between them.

Sean carried on, touching her fingers. "She's perfect. We had placed a call to this organization that collects donated breast milk and Randy went to pick up some. She's a good eater."

I stared at my niece, my sweet beautiful niece. Her head had rounded out a bit, and her hair wasn't as dark as it had been.

As if he read my curiosity, Randy said, "They gave her a bath." He pulled out his phone and thumbed across his screen. "Want to see pics?"

"I'm good." My nose to the top of her head, I breathed in that fresh baby smell.

"She's gorgeous," Korey said from behind me as he placed a hand on my shoulder. "Shayne was a little shy on details."

"Well…" Sean grabbed a piece of paper. "We forgot to ask, but the nurse gave us this." He held up a pink card with the birth details. "She was born at 9:47 am, weighs 6lbs 15oz, and is 21.75 inches long."

"Tall, skinny thing, eh?" Korey laughed.

My brother and brother-in-law exchanges glances and Sean asked, "Want to know her name?"

I nodded.

"Scarlett Shayne Jasmina."

Wow! "You named her after me?" I gave my namesake a tender squeeze.

"Yeah, your name is in there. As is Randy's grandma."

My brows furrowed. "I didn't know her name was Jasmina?"

"It wasn't." Randy laughed. "It was Scarlett."

"I don't know what to say." I was so surprised. Honoured, really. I spoke to my namesake, "I'm going to be the best aunty ever." As it dawned on me how she had my name and not my sister's, I looked at my brother. "Dina will flip, you know."

"Whatever. I can handle it," Sean said with a smile and a dismissive wave. "As much as I love her, I don't want a child with a name as old as hers."

"Where does Jasmina come from then?" I stroked my niece's cheek and she turned her head toward my finger. A couple of seconds later, she started fussing.

"I'd better take her back," Randy said, reaching for his daughter. Like an expert, he had her cradled and settled in his arms in a heartbeat. "It's JodiLynn's middle name."

"Cool," I said. "It's nice she has a part of the name."

"Isn't he good?" Sean asked, never taking his eyes off the pair. He leaned his head against Randy's bicep and smiled down on his daughter.

I was dying to know the answer to a question I hadn't heard anyone ask yet. "How is she? JodiLynn?"

Randy nodded and swallowed, gently swaying and rocking. "Good. Resting. We've asked if we can see her, but she refuses. The social worker came by, and she signed off on everything. However…" Randy swallowed and turned his back.

"She still has ten days to change her mind." Sean filled in the rest of the details. Adoption could be so tricky, even after getting your baby.

"Oh." I looked between the men and new dads. "Is that a possibility?"

Sean paced in the small space. "Not likely, considering she'd refused to see Scarlett."

Randy held his daughter a little tighter. "But you never know."

"We'll wait, and in ten days, we'll see."

God, ten days. That would feel like a lifetime especially with the uncertainty that the birth mother could request her baby back at any time, for any reason, within those days. "Can I see her? JodiLynn I mean?"

Sean cleared his throat, and Scarlett startled. "Sorry, baby girl." He rocked on his heels. "I think, we think…" He wiggled a finger between him and Randy. "It's best if you don't."

Randy piped up. "It sounds completely selfish, but we don't want to spoil our chances and have her change her mind."

I nodded my understanding. I didn't want to be the reason for her to possibly change her mind either. "Okay." Still, I wanted to see if she was okay and coping with the drastic changes in her body as the books and videos showed how tough those first few days could be. It would be scary to deal with them alone; however, I'd abide by their wishes, and I guess hers too, and leave her be.

Scarlett let go and a deep bubbly sound rumbled around her bottom.

"It's my turn," Sean said, grabbing a fresh diaper and cloth. He spread a thick blanket on the bed and set up a mini change station.

I turned my head and glanced over to Korey, who stood beside me like a statue. "And that's my cue. She's cute and all, but I already change enough diapers with Jordan. I'm good for now."

"Are you sure?" Randy asked, uncovering the baby.

Her legs were so scrawny and red tinted. She really was a long, thin baby.

I gave a quick wave and pushed Korey towards the exit with my good hand. "Yeah, have fun."

"We're going to Mom and Dad's tomorrow after we get discharged. Well, after she gets discharged. Why don't you come out?"

"When?" I had a list a mile long I needed to get through, but if it happened to be in the afternoon between Jordan and Westside…

"Late morning."

There went that plan. "I'm working. But I'll be coming by for regular visits. You can count on it." I linked fingers with Korey. "Have fun."

Stealing a quick peek at my niece I closed the door behind us, and we walked in silence down the hall. Around us, the cries of newborns echoed out into the hall and nurses and white coats shuffled around us. Many babies were getting a fresh start, you could almost feel it in the air. "You were quiet in there."

Korey shrugged and gripped my hand. "Babies aren't my thing, but she's a definite keeper."

A wild smile took centre stage on my face. "Isn't she? I hope the ten days pass quickly, and nothing happens that takes Scarlett away from them."

"Me too."

"I don't even want to think about what they'd be like if their dream was taken away. I know if it were me and someone claimed my baby, I'd be beside myself." Losing something so precious would cause a wound so deep. I shuddered. Hopefully, everything ends up going well for them. "Do you see yourself with kids someday?" I imagined myself with at least a half-dozen kids, all piling on top of me, and playing and laughing.

High on the thought, the elevator dinged and we squeezed ourselves into the crowd of people and rode down. I kept looking at Korey, but his lips stayed firmly shut. Not a word, not a mumble, not even the start of a mumble. On the main floor, the doors opened, and the flood of people escaped out from around us.

Holding my hand, we stepped out and circled past the crowd waiting to board.

"You never answered my question." I pulled him to a stop

beside the gift shop where bright blooms sat on top of glass shelves. "About kids."

"I hadn't forgot the question. I just don't think this is the right time to discuss it."

"Really? I think it's the perfect time. Just like at funerals you discuss death and the what ifs, being surrounded by fresh babies is the perfect time."

He resumed walking, but this time without me. I couldn't believe how he ignored my question. Unless he thought—

"Wait." I called out and ran to catch up. "In case you're wondering, I wasn't thinking you and me go and procreate tomorrow or anything. Our relationship is way too new for that." I reached out to hold his hand. It was tense and fought with me as I tried to uncurl it.

"Good, because I'm not ready for that."

I looked up into his eyes, desperate to make sure I conveyed that feeling as well. "Nor am I. I'm barely an adult." Barely. I still had so much debt I needed to clear away and schooling to pay for. Having a baby right now would be an epic disaster.

He thumbed toward the hospital. "Yeah, well that little girl up there just did a very adult thing."

My hand rested on his chest. "I know. And in many ways, she's light years more mature than me, because I don't know if I could do it. Give up a baby."

"You don't have to be a child to give up a child. It can happen at any age, you know." His voice pitched and lowered, and he started walking away from me again. But this time, it wasn't out of anger. It was out of hurt.

Was he trying to tell me something without really telling me? Gee, guys can be so elusive in admitting they have feelings. Within a couple of steps, I caught up and I looped my arm through his. "Whatever you want to tell me, I'll listen to. I'm here for you."

"I know."

"Is it about your mom?" I took a stab in the dark, but it

seemed the most logical. He'd mentioned his father but never his mother. Not once.

"If and when I want to discuss Pamela, I will. Until then, this conversation is over." The firmness in his voice sent a chill up and down my back. I'd hit the nail with the hammer on that one. Ouch. "By the way, don't forget to call Lily back."

Yeah, I'd noticed how many times she called me, and the voicemail messages she'd left. Figuring it would be quicker to call her from the car where I hoped to avoid a lengthy phone call, I dialled.

The phone rang twice before she answered. "Shayne, I'm so sorry. I'm a terrible drunk who becomes a mean friend."

I didn't know how to reply to that, so I nodded, and with the edge of my sore hand, pushed my glasses up.

"Really, I hope for the best between you and Korey, and I shouldn't have dumped my marital woes on you." She sounded apologetic, and I wanted to forgive her, but I wasn't ready yet.

"Did you talk to Jason about it?" I bit my tongue to keep from barking out, but I was suddenly mad.

"No."

"Lily."

"I know." Her voice fell. "But I needed to make amends with you first. When I woke up this morning, I felt terrible. In every way that a person could feel terrible. And I called and called, and you didn't answer, so then I felt worse. I figured you were ignoring me."

Good. My tongue was getting sore from the biting. "I was at the hospital."

"For the baby I hope?"

"Yeah, I'm just leaving now." I looked over at Korey who remained stoic-faced as he sat in the driver seat.

"Well, I'm glad your brother has his baby now."

A smile replaced the frown. "Me too." I fiddled with the hem of my shorts, folding and unfolding it as the air between Lily and I thickened like pea soup.

"I really am sorry, Shayne. Please forgive me."

"Okay."

A spring of hope in her voice. "Okay, you'll forgive me?"

"Yeah." But I didn't know if I meant it just yet. "But you really need to talk to Jason. Especially if you're seriously thinking of leaving him."

The air crackled between us. "I'll let you go. Get some sleep, and we'll plan a get together soon so I can hear all the gory birth details."

"Sure, goodbye." I leaned against the head rest and tossed my phone into the cup holder. Twisting my head around, I stared at Korey.

"Everything's all good?"

"I suppose. She didn't sound like herself though, but maybe I'm just tired."

He brought my hand up to his lips and brushed a sweet kiss over my knuckles. "Let's get you home and put you to bed."

"I like the sound of that."

Chapter Fourteen

"No bandage tonight?" Evanora asked as she waltzed by with a trayful of drinks.

I waved my healed hand in the air. "Nope. Doctor said I'm good to go." A few days were long enough. It was hard to play with Jordan when I couldn't properly catch a ball, although it did make him laugh more when I missed. The bruised hand made it harder, but not impossible, to serve drinks and such. But the worst was the damper it put in my lovemaking. Now I could throw caution to the wind and be as wild as I wanted.

"And there go your pity tips." She pushed past me as a morsel of truth hung in the air.

It had been nice—the pity tips as she called them. People loved hearing how my hand got damaged, and I loved telling them about the whole birth mother, gay couple, adoption story. Each recap excited me further, especially when I mentioned the beauty of birth and that magical first cry.

"You should look into becoming a doula," one customer told me. "My daughter used one at her birth."

I didn't know much about that, but it was something I'd check out when I got home. The more the customer went on about it, the more excited I got. And suddenly, my shift couldn't end soon enough.

Despite what Evanora had said, my tips were still decent. Maybe that's because the smile hadn't left my face all evening. So far, my shift had been easy and no screw ups on my part.

Jasper popped his head into the server station as I made a fresh pot of coffee. "Party of three, B6."

"Thanks." Grabbing my tray of drinks for another table, I dropped them off and made my way to the new table, all while keeping my eye on Jasper, who was laughing loudly at one of his tables and clapping the customer on the shoulder.

Turning to face B6, I froze. There he smugly sat in the booth with a couple of guys I didn't recognize. Fear turned my blood ice cold and my stomach into a tangled knot. Before I could walk away, he spotted me, and an evil-looking grin spread across his face and he elbowed the guy beside him. Like a scared child, I dashed back into the server station.

"Evanora, can you take B6?" It was close enough to her section that she could easily take it on.

"Nope. One of those guys specifically asked to sit in your section."

Shit. This was going to be a long night. Maybe Korey would take the table. I held my breath for a moment as I waited for him to return to the station.

"Hey, Jasper," I said, slowly and seductively. I wasn't as skilled with the charm and flirtatious nature as he was, but I had to try. "Can you take the guys at B6?" The table was out of his way, but you never knew. I batted my lashes for extra effect.

"Can't. Just got slammed with a group." Glasses of pop filled his tray along with a couple cold beers.

Well, there went that.

Swallowing my trepidation, I approached the table cautiously. "Hi, I'm Jade, I'll be your server tonight. What can I get you?" I glanced around the table but refused to make contact with him.

Two beers and an iced tea.

"Aren't you, Shayne Davenport? From West Grove High?" he asked me.

My knees went weak and I worried they'd give out on me,

but I tried to keep my composure. "No, I'm Jade." I pointed at my nametag for effect. Stepping back, I said, "I'll be right back with your drinks."

On my way to the server station, distracted by the table I'd rather not serve, I ran into Evanora, sending a basket of bread flying.

"Oh, I'm so sorry." I bent down to pick up the debris off the floor.

"You're such a–" But she stopped. "You're supposed to come in that way. Through there." She pointed with an angry finger to the far entrance which I knew, but the one I was currently hunched inside was closer to my escape.

"I'm really sorry." The basket in my hand, I tossed the no-good bread into the waste, and set the basket into a bussing tray.

"Get bent," she said, fetching a fresh basket and hollering at the cook. "I need another six." She spun in my direction. "Stay away from me. You're bad news."

What? I stepped back, out into the open and for some stupid reason, I checked the one table I'd rather not serve. They were in direct line of sight, and I was being watched. By *him.* The knotted mess in my stomach started to grow and fester, and my hands trembled as I poured their drinks.

My tray felt as unbalanced as my wobbly walk back to their table. With as much grace as I could muster, I set their drinks down and took their order. The two strange guys paid me no attention, thank goodness, so I walked over to another one of my tables as the hair prickled on the back of my head, I just knew I was being watched.

A minute later I served a different table with their bill and he cornered me. In attempt to stay away, I backed up into the wall.

"Who would've thought Little Miss Priss would be working a lowly waitressing job?" He wasn't touching me—after the last time, he knew better—but he was uncomfortably close. Breath I hoped to never smell again wafted around me, bringing flashbacks to the surface. "Tonight's going to be so much fun."

"You stay away from me." My voice was shaky.

I knew it and he did too as he gave me a once-over, a slow lingering gaze that made my insides flip upside down and caused a thrust of adrenaline to pulse through my body. "I like it when a girl's nervous. It makes it all the more exciting."

The air cooled all around me, and my stomach gave another flip. "Excuse me," I said, stepping around him, careful to not touch him in any way. My fingers pounded against the screen as I punched his table's order, wave after relentless wave of nausea rolling in my stomach. Moving quickly, I rushed to the back of the building, into the staff change rooms, and threw up my supper into the garbage. I didn't even make it to the toilet.

Each clench of my stomach brought back a fresh wave of memories, none of them pleasant.

Of Ben, drinking way too much at my cousin's wedding.

Of a midnight walk out into the field of wheat for some fresh air and stargazing.

Of hands violently digging into my privates when he pushed me to the ground.

My screams were stifled by the feel of a rough hand across my mouth until someone bigger and stronger pulled him off, threatening him within an inch of his life.

Randy held me tightly until my tears stopped and helped me clean up and fix my messy hair laden with straw and grass. I begged him not to tell another living soul what he stumbled upon. But I was thankful, so thankful he showed up when he did for things could've been so much worse. The *R* word flashed in my brain like a neon sign. And when we walked back into the hall, no one was the wiser, and the only explanation given was Ben left in a hurry due to a family emergency. Because, according to Randy, he'd never have a family if he so much as laid another finger on me.

When I got back to my apartment, he used my spare key and stole the money I'd hidden to pay rent was gone. My backup cash for crisis was also gone, and the drawer it was taped to destroyed. And as I later found out, he'd stolen my car and involved it in a hit and run accident, which cost me thousands of dollars and a rise in insurance premiums.

Feeling empty, I washed my face and sat down on the lid of the toilet, leaning my head against the divider, the cool of the metal welcome on my heated cheeks. After a few calming breaths, I slowly inched my way over to my locker where I pulled out my phone and sent a quick text to Randy.

He's here. At Westside.

It didn't take long for him to respond. *I'll be there in ten. You okay?*

Yes and no, but please don't come. Our deal was that I tell you.

Yeah? Try and stop me.

And as much as I didn't want to, I smiled. After that horrible night, in order for Randy to keep the situation quiet, it was imperative I told him of any encounter with Ben.

Still nauseated but feeling a tad more in control, I powdered my face and locked up my locker. Resuming my job, I delivered steak bowls and other foods to my three other tables, trying to avoid Ben's at all costs.

"You okay?" Jasper asked upon my return. "You've lost all your colour."

Part of me was mad at him that he wouldn't help me out and I had to deal with Ben on my own and the other part was mad at the part that was already mad, because I hadn't given him a reason for why I didn't want that table. If I had explained, maybe he would've. I was mad at Jasper for something that was my fault, but I barked at him anyway. "Just peachy."

I stormed back out into the dining room.

"Ah, miss," one of Ben's tablemates hollered out.

I stopped and turned in their direction. "Yes?" I said in a voice so sweet I should've had cavities.

"I'd like another beer."

"Sure thing."

I wanted to spit into his beer, or do something evil, but I

didn't have it in me. Besides, I didn't want to get fired if I got caught. Instead, like the good girl I was, I poured it and presented it to him. When I headed back towards the station, my eyes went wide in delight and a tiny smile festered at the edge of my lips.

Randy stood at the entrance.

Jasper beat me to him. "Hey, Randy," he said, shifting a small stack of menus. "What brings you by?"

He narrowed his eyes at Jasper, focusing briefly on the name tag.

"Here I'm called Jasper."

"Ah." Randy nodded and locked eyes with me, before searching over my shoulder. "Newborns never give you much time to eat so I'm here to grab us some hot food." He winked at me and walked up to the till.

Jasper hopped onto the other side of the counter. "What'll you have?"

I stood beside Randy, trying to calm myself. A sharp inhale of air did nothing to sooth my frazzled nerves. "Today's special is the Peppered Riki."

Randy scanned the restaurant, but Ben's table was out of our line of sight. "Good gawd, no. Nothing spicy." His eyes fell to the takeout menu I handed him. "Give me a Montreal Bowl and a Lotus bowl, with a basket of bread too. Please." He added as an afterthought.

Jasper rang in Randy's order. "Give it about ten minutes."

"That's fine." He nodded and puffed his chest out. "Excuse me, I think I see someone I know."

"No problem. I'll be right back." Jasper disappeared into the back.

I got a pat on the back as Randy inched by me. "You know, you didn't have to come." I looked up into my brother-in-law's eyes.

Randy looked down on me, stretching up to his full height. Even though he was a true pussycat, his form was very threatening. "Oh, I think I needed to. What did he do?"

I quietly, while constantly checking to make sure no one was listening, gave him a play by play. "But he never touched me." I don't know why I added that. Maybe because I didn't want a scene. Especially a scene that would possibly involve me. Being the recipient of attention never worked out in my favour.

"B6," the cook yelled out, unaware I stood three feet away.

"'Scuse me." I grabbed the three steak bowls and another basket of bread.

"It's been a few months. Time to jog someone's memory," Randy whispered just steps behind me.

As I approached Ben's table, he looked over. And paled. He wiggled in his seat, trapped between the wall and his buddy.

I set down their food and smiled.

Randy was a quietly intimidating guy. If his muscles didn't frighten you, then his words did. He'd dealt with some psychopathic clientele and knew just the right thing to say.

"Can I get you anything else?" My eyes focused on Ben.

All the guys, except Ben, shook their heads and dug in. He sat there with his tail tucked between his legs like a frightened little dog. I hoped he remembered that feeling of fear for the rest of his life because it was the same fear and revulsion I got whenever I thought of him.

Randy shooshed me away and I went back to check on my other tables while keeping a firm eye on him. He didn't make a scene, but several low growls rolled out of him and the guy on Ben's right also paled. Whatever Randy said, I'll never know.

As a small token of my appreciation I paid for his meals and thanked him as he left with the brown bag full of hot food.

"Let me know if he does or says *anything*." Randy placed a quick peck on my cheek and took off.

It wasn't long after Randy left that Ben and his buddies took off. Just as well, waiting on them left more than just a sour taste in my mouth. My body quivered and shook, and I needed a shower desperately to wipe away his presence. I hoped I'd never have to run into that nasty guy ever again.

The restaurant locked its doors and Jasper and I sat around the staff table, just the two of us. Evanora had left already, having cashed out earlier in the night.

My fear had dissolved, and I felt bad for being mad at Jasper for something he didn't do or had no clue what had gone on. "Sorry I snapped at you earlier."

"Yeah about that." A half smile appeared, and he unwrapped his apron and tossed it on the seat beside him. "Want to tell me what's going on? Every time I tried to talk to you, you brushed me off or ignored me completely."

"My mind was someplace else." I shook my head and lowered my gaze. If I never had to repeat that memory, it would still be too soon.

"I sensed it wasn't the place where you and I were–"

Niall interrupted the remainder of that sentence as he strode over with the envelopes. "Well, the winner of the highest paid tip award goes to you." He tossed me my payout for the evening. "I photocopied the bill for you. Good job."

Curious, I ripped it open and pulled out the paper. The bill was from Ben's table, the tip amount highlighted. One hundred and twenty-five dollars. My hands started shaking, and I glanced up to Niall. "Is this a joke? It'll bounce you know."

"I double checked with the customer, and he confirmed it. Then to be sure, I processed it." He tapped me on the shoulders and headed back to his office.

"What's going on?" Jasper twisted in confusion. The paper rattled as I passed it over. Jasper's eyes got bigger. "Wow! That's a nice payout."

"It's payback, but I'll take it." *$125 down, $3000 more to go before he's zeroed out that financial debt he caused.* Inside I was smiling though. However little in the grand scheme of things this was, it was something. And it probably killed Ben to do it, even if he was likely threatened to have done it.

Jasper's shoulders rolled forward and he slouched against

the back of the booth. "You're not going to tell me, are you?"

I pushed my glasses up and stared straight ahead. It wasn't much to look at, but it was better than seeing hurt and agitation on the one beside me. "It's a long story, and it makes me a little ill thinking of it."

"That table…" He tapped the bill between his fingers and moved a little closer to me. "Is that the one you asked me to cover?"

"Yeah," I sighed. Wonder flitted around inside me. Was he jealous? Did he think if he took that table that the tip would've been his?

"Does it have anything to do with Randy being here?"

I should've known better that my boyfriend wasn't self-centered, just a caring guy. Inside me, the rumblings of a super jerk grew. I was a major idiot.

"An ex-boyfriend that burned you?" His voice oozed with curiosity and concern.

"That he was." My head turned to the main entrance, keeping Jasper to the back of my head. "Randy interrupted an attempt--" I couldn't even say it. The words choked me, suffocating me the way Ben's hand once did.

He slid right beside me, and gently wrapped an arm around me.

I swallowed down the hurt rising in me. "And then he stole my money and my car."

"That makes better sense why Randy was here, although his excuse was valid too."

"I texted him from the bathroom after the jerk privately confronted me." Burning bile inched up my throat and nausea took centre stage in the pit of my stomach.

"You should've said something."

"I tried." Still unable to face him, I lowered my head on my arm.

His hand rubbed from my shoulder to my fingertips and back up again, warming me up. I was surprised how cold I suddenly felt. "Yes, you did now that I think about it. I'm sorry I wasn't more attentive."

"I'm sorry I got mad at you for not understanding."

He laughed, a rumbling, throat-clearing laugh. "Next time, be more direct. I'm a guy. Subtlety never works on me."

"I promise to try."

Chapter Fifteen

"Are you sleeping?" I whispered and rolled over, draping my arm around Korey's strong abs. Even in the middle of the night, they were taut and rippled. And hairless. That made me giggle considering all the hair he had on his head.

He grunted. "Maybe."

I nuzzled into his back, pulling my body closer. "Go back to sleep."

"Well, that'll help." The bed bounced as he shifted. "It's two-thirty."

"I know."

"Did I not wear you out?" Even in the pitch black I could see the smile growing. He snaked an arm under me and I snuggled into his shoulder.

"It's not that."

"Lily still on your mind?"

It had been a little strange to get a phone call from Lily on a Saturday morning. Especially so early on a Saturday morning. She claimed she found one of Jordan's toys in the diaper bag from a playdate earlier in the week. It was so important that she give it back today. In my sleepy haze I agreed and met her at my door ten minutes later.

Lily was frazzled and her hair all a mess, eyeliner smudged like she slept in her makeup and woke up to run out of the house.

She hadn't even had the decency to brush her teeth and the morning breath that hit me was enough to knock me flat on my ass.

I asked Korey, "Wasn't that whole thing weird?"

"I honestly couldn't tell you, but I'd believe you if you said it was." He covered a yawn.

"I just can't stop thinking about it. It's like she was frantic, high almost. Do you think she's using drugs?"

A shoulder moved under my head. "Call her in the morning. Maybe she had one too many espresso shots."

"Maybe." Something about her attitude didn't feel right to me. I couldn't put my finger on what it was though. Instead of letting it bother me more, I drew a heart with my finger on Korey's chest. "Distract me. Tell me something about you that I don't know. Tell me about your upbringing."

"Let's not."

"Why not? You know lots about me." It had taken a lot out of me to give him the details surrounding everything with Ben. "I want to know more about you."

He sighed, and his body crumpled beside me.

I wanted to know more, and since he wasn't going to answer much, I was going to jump to conclusions. "Was it traumatic?"

"No. It's just complicated. So unfairly complicated." Another sigh caused his chest to cave with the exhale.

"Ooh, I love a good drama." I cozied up closer. "I promise to reveal something juicy on my family tree when you're done."

It came out almost like a snort. "You've got something juicy? Why don't I believe it?"

"Stop changing the subject." I swatted his chest. "Tell me about yours."

His fingers twirled in my hair. "Fine." A long, lingering sigh. "You see, my birth mother had me at a young age, not as young as JodiLynn was. I'd been told she was seventeen or so, but, regardless, she gave me up. It was a closed adoption so not much is known about her or the sperm donor or biological father. Tony and Pamela adopted me and I was their only child. But Tony wasn't a great husband, and a worse father, and he left us when I was four. I have no idea what became of him, and I don't care."

I shuddered a little. Korey's tone was angry.

"See? You're already bothered, and I've barely begun."

He pulled away from me, but I wrapped my arm around him to tell him he wasn't leaving. Good, bad or otherwise, I was holding on tight. "Please, continue. I want to know."

"Pamela wasn't a much better parent, but we made do. She home-schooled me—sporadically—while we worked on her dad's—Harry's—farm. Pamela remarried a guy named Marcus just before my eleventh birthday, and suddenly we were this weird, little family. I didn't even know what to call Marcus, but step-dad seemed to work. Well Pamela decided a few months later that she'd had enough of the farming life, of being a shitty mother, of responsibility in general, and took off. No goodbye, no warning, nothing. She went into the farmhouse to make us lunch and when we came in, a note was on our sandwiches. She walked away. Literally. Aside from a missing suitcase, it was like she was still there. And for months we expected her to walk back into the kitchen like nothing ever happened." He paused and caught his breath.

I wondered if it felt as good for him to share it as it did for me to hear it. Finally, I got an insight into his life. "That had to be rough." My heart broke for him. How awful. And here I thought my family was weird and dysfunctional, and yet we were more textbook than anything else.

"She never came back. So Marcus, in conjunction with Harry, who felt he wasn't schooled enough to teach me, enrolled me in the local community school, where I failed miserably, naturally. It's hard to fit in when you're different and you know nothing and are grades below other kids the same age. However, with the help of a great teacher, I caught up to my peers. It took me two years, but when I started high school, I was on par with the rest of them."

"Wow, that's great. Yay for your teachers." I couldn't believe my ears with what he shared. Until he was a young man, he had no solid upbringing. None. But his step-dad must've taught him more than just educational things because Korey was kind and sweet, and with the way he grew up, I'd expect him to be bitter and conniving.

"Yeah," he said, his voice lacking emotion. "I graduated as a 'C' student, which didn't open a lot of doors but whatever. Marcus offered to pull some strings for me and get a job at the bank he worked at, but I wasn't interested. Nothing in that small town held any future for me. I felt stifled there. A month after graduation, I left. But at least I warned everybody and kept in contact. I still do. But I haven't been back there since."

"And then you moved here?"

"I slowly made my way east." A loose smile inched from his lips.

"Where have you lived?"

His chest rose and fell, and I snuggled in closer.

"Well, I've lived in Kelowna, and worked on the ski hill in Big White. That was a lot of fun. But Jasper was pretty cool too. Gotta love the mountains."

I remembered that a while back, he'd listed all the places he lived. At the time, I thought it was all the places since he was born, not since he graduated from high school a few years back. "And what made you decide to move here?" I didn't mean to have any disgust in my voice because I loved my city for its small town like atmosphere, I just couldn't imagine someone purposely moving here from someplace as beautiful and breathtaking as the mountains.

"It was time to change scenery. Explore something new."

"Do you do that often?" I swallowed down a morsel of incoming panic. "Explore something new?"

"Yeah. Depends on whatever lease I've signed."

"What did you sign when you moved here?"

"A year. Thought I'd try out a longer term. Most other places were six months."

I didn't want to ask *when* he signed it, for fear the upcoming date would be soon. The idea that he would want to just up and leave started to make a morsel of sense. His minimalist apartment, the lack of a secure job. Surely one could get a serving position in any city or town. It's not like that would be too difficult.

Yawning, I wrapped a leg around his and nuzzled my nose against the crook of his neck while his fingers lazily twirled in my hair. We lay there for a while, the breaths stretching out longer and longer into the night. I envied that, as with all the new information he shared, I had no idea how I was going to get to sleep now.

Sleep did find me for when I woke up, the sunlight had brightened the room, the white of the walls more barren than before. Grabbing one of his t-shirts, which incidentally barely covered my ass, I sauntered down the hallway. Korey—in all his naked glory—stood in the kitchen chowing down on a bowl of Shreddies.

"Morning, sleeping beauty."

"Morning," I mumbled.

"You're not supposed to wear clothes to breakfast, you know."

I nodded. It had become routine but for some reason after last night, I didn't want to feel so naked and exposed.

"However, you're sexy as hell in my shirt, so I'll let it fly." He held out a mug. "Coffee?"

"No thanks."

For a moment, he seemed offended, but set the mug down and instead poured me a glass of milk.

I sat at the table, holding the cool glass, unable to make eye contact. Instead, I slowly swirled my drink and watched as the few milky bubbles sailed around the rim.

"Want something to eat?"

"No thanks. I'll grab something while I'm out."

He slumped into the seat across from me, and reached out his hand, tipping up my chin.

"Where are you going?"

"Over to Sean and Randy's. Need my baby fix."

"Can I come? It's been a while since I've seen her, and them."

I shrugged, wondering where the desire to see a baby came from, especially when he said he wasn't into them. "I guess."

He narrowed his eyes at me and dropped his hand. "You okay?"

"Just tired," I said, taking a sip. The milk was extra cold this morning, borderline frosty.

"Something's on your mind."

There were many things I contemplated but I wasn't sure which one to give a voice to. My focus remained on the glass as the thoughts swirled, hoping for clarity in the confusion. So much I couldn't understand like the lack of love he didn't get growing up. His inability to stay anywhere for any length of time. His apparent passion for me. It pained me how different we were, and yet, try as I did, I couldn't unravel myself from him. "I love you." It just rolled off my tongue and straight out my mouth before I knew what it was doing. We hadn't said that yet to each other, and this probably wasn't the time. At least not the right time.

"I'm flattered."

And there in his response to my total honesty lay the truth. No quick I love you too reply because he didn't feel the same way about me. He leaned back against his chair, his face a blank state. Each passing second, my heart splinted a little more. Was that part of his plan? Waltz into town, bed the local naïve one and drift on out like a storm? Did he have someone like me in every place he visited? Was I a long-term notch in the proverbial bed post?

I sighed, and hearing nothing further from him, I quickly changed and headed towards home. Alone. But I didn't make it all the way there, instead I found myself pulling up in front of Sean and Randy's house earlier than I had expected. I was going to call first, after a shower and a nap. However, I needed to be with them. With my family.

Sitting in my car, I sat and stared wondering what my future held. I banged the steering wheel and accidentally hit the horn, its loud beep echoing in the cul-de-sac. Shifting down in my seat and covering my face, I hid. My phone buzzed beside me on the passenger seat. It was Sean.

Are you coming in or are you going to stay out there all day?

I picked up the phone and debated.

Don't make me come out there. I'm in my jammies.

Feet on the ground, I forced myself up the front walk to the entrance where a frazzled Sean stood in pajamas he had to have had since high school. They were thread bare and sported a jungle themed print that no one should wear.

"Shh," he whispered and ushered me in, closing the door behind me. "What brings you by to stalk my house so early on a Sunday?"

The house was eerily quiet. Usually a radio played in the background and there was idle chatter. All I heard was the humming from a small table top fan. I kept my voice low, "Man troubles."

"Are there any other kind?" He laughed a gentle laugh.

I gave my brother another once over. "What's with the terrible choice in clothing?"

"It was all I had clean. Scarlett dirtied the others."

I narrowed my eyes. "Okay."

"It's probably best we leave it at that."

We tiptoed into the living room. The leather chair squeaked as I sat, and my eyes popped open as a result. "Sorry."

He dismissed it with a wave as he walked across the living room. It wasn't a big space but sizeable enough to hold a couch, a loveseat and a chair along with a giant-sized fish tank. "So what happened?"

"I blurted out I love you, and he said he was flattered."

"Ouch." Sean sat on the couch, tucking his feet under a blanket.

"I'm so stupid." One of the fish stared at me. I swear it looked like it nodded in agreement.

"Why?"

"I shouldn't have said that."

"I assumed when you said the whole 'I blurted it out' part it wasn't supposed to have happened." Sean winked. "But what's wrong with loving him?"

I picked at my fingernails, pushing my cuticles back and scraping the raised skin around the nail beds. "Several reason really. When we started together I didn't want any attachment, just a little fun. I have college in the fall. I didn't want to be tied down so I could experience everything. But somewhere, things changed and well… feelings started forming. Then last night he informed me he doesn't stay in one place very long. He prefers to try a new adventure every six months to a year."

He raised his brows at me, the whites of his eyes getting larger. "And?"

"He signed a year's lease here and I think it's coming up soon."

"But you don't know?" It was soft and quiet, but I heard the chortle in his laugh.

"No."

"Did you ask?"

"I'm afraid."

"Because?"

"Of the whole falling in love with him part." I hugged my legs and rested my chin on my knees. My glasses slid down my nose and I pushed them back up.

Footsteps slapped on the kitchen floor and Randy poked his head around their feature wall which separated the living room from the kitchen. "Oh, good morning. Was wondering who was in here."

"Shayne was just telling me that she said those three words to Korey and he responded with, what was it?"

"I'm flattered," I deadpanned.

Sean carried on. "And he's a bit of a drifter so she worried about what this will do because she's falling for him." He faced me. "That about right?"

I nodded and buried my face between my knees.

"Sounds like we're going to need expressos and twice baked." Randy disappeared behind the wall.

"What's that?"

Sean whispered, "Biscotti, but he can never say it properly, so he calls it twice baked."

Scarlett's wee cries pierced the air. "I'll get her." Sean jumped from the couch and went to go get his daughter.

I walked into the kitchen. A fancy unit stood on the counter, to which Randy dropped in a bottle of milk and pushed a button. Beside the sink were a variety of bottles, soothers and a can of formula. Also, a bottle of wine and a couple of glasses. As much as the baby stuff dominated, it was good to see they hadn't changed much.

Randy waved a bottle under my face, snapping me out of my own private world. "You're really in love with him, eh?"

"I really am." In saying it, my heart responded and jumped up to adrenaline fueled levels. It pounded against my rib cage, in perfect rhythm. Kor-ey. Kor-ey. I swore my heart beat his name.

"Scared?"

I looked up into Randy's eyes, which were staring back at me, piercing right into the brutal honest truth. "Never been more scared."

He squeezed my forearm and pointed at the cupboard. "Grab me the espresso cups, please." I passed him a white one and he shook his head. "The espresso cups are the little ones. They're behind those."

Finding the right ones, I handed him three.

He placed all three on a serving tray, along with a plate of biscotti.

Scarlett's cries became stronger.

"That girl loves to eat." He tapped his finger against the bottle warmer.

The cries became louder as Sean walked into the kitchen. "Ready yet?" He gazed at the bottle.

"Soon." Randy kissed Scarlett's red forehead. "Good morning, Sunshine."

Sean bounced his screaming newborn around the kitchen, and Randy grabbed the tray of drinks and cookies. I followed him into the living room and resumed my seat. It was hard to hear myself think over the wails. Who knew a baby could be so loud? A toddler I expected, and Jordan often was, but a baby?

Finally, the racket stopped when the bottle warmer beeped, and Sean started feeding his little girl.

"Ah," Randy said, echoing my previous thoughts. "There's nothing wrong with her lungs."

"Nothing at all." I agreed and reached for a steaming cup of espresso. Not a coffee fan at all, but there was something about it. I think it was the cream he added to mine, and a spoonful of sugar. So it probably wasn't remotely close to an espresso at all, but at least it was tolerable.

Randy recounted the past two nights of endless crying on Scarlett's part. "Newborns are lovable, but man are they tough."

Sean sat beside his spouse. "So trying, but so worth it. Would you look at that face?"

Randy beamed. "Best gift ever." And he planted a peck on Sean's cheek.

It never bothered me, all their signs of affection with each other and how they were so open about it. I'm glad they were confident enough in their relationship to let the world know. I envied that because as much as I did love Korey, I wasn't sure I was ready for the world to know. It had been shocking enough to let him know and his reaction was earth shattering.

"Court date tomorrow?" I searched their faces. The ten days was almost up. Officially, if JodiLynn cancelled her parenting rights, or whatever it was called, Sean and Randy would be Scarlett's legal parents.

"We meet with the family lawyer at nine-fifteen." Sean focused all his attention on the sweet baby bundled in his arms.

"And by nine-thirty, she'll legally be ours."

Aww, they were so close. Less than twenty-four hours to go.

"So," Sean said, returning his focus in my direction. "What are you going to do about lover boy?"

"I don't know."

"You really need to talk to him. Only he can answer the questions you have." Randy raised his brow. "Do you think you could follow him?"

"You mean, if he decided to up and move away?" I hadn't thought about it. I just figured he wouldn't want me to, that I was something fun he had once. I'd be the connection to this city. Oh god, was that how he referred to the other girls? Ginger from Jasper, Trish from Kelowna? I didn't know if those were his former girlfriend's names or not, but now I couldn't stop wondering. Is that what he thought? Thinking about him moving on without me made the cracks in my heart grow into crevasses. I was falling so hard for this guy, and it was painfully obvious.

My phone rang from the pocket of my sweater. Korey's name flashed on the screen. I tucked it back into my pocket.

"Go ahead and answer it, we don't mind," Randy said, giving Scarlett's exposed foot a tender rub.

"Maybe she wants some privacy?" Sean whispered.

I shook my head. "It's not that at all. I just don't know what to say or do."

Sean pulled the empty bottle away. "Well avoiding him isn't the solution."

I curled up into the leather chair and rested my head back on my knees while I studied the guys purring over their daughter.

Randy and Sean had a rough start to their relationship, but once they talked to each other, things improved. "I know. And I'll figure it out. I just need time to think."

"Well if you think he's going to up and take off soon, you might not have as much time as you'd like to debate and war with yourself over whether you would go or stay." Randy lifted Scarlett and placed her against his shoulder. After a few taps on the back, she released her pent-up air. "That's my sweet baby girl."

And that was the kicker. How much time *did* I have? Would Korey leave when his lease ended? Would he renew? If he left, would he ask me to go with him? Did he feel strong enough about me to even consider asking, or was I really just a notch? And if he did ask me, would I be able to go? So many questions and zero answers.

Chapter Sixteen

After all the baby snuggles and espresso I could handle which wasn't much on either front, I bid adieu to my brother and brother-in-law and headed to my apartment. As soon as I called Korey, he agreed to come over and was knocking on my door before I had a chance to clean up. Had he been parked in the parking lot just waiting?

I opened the door. Dreads thick as a finger peaked over the top of an embarrassingly large display of daisies, roses and something pink I couldn't remember the name of. "What are those for?"

He lowered and passed them to me. "They're an apology."

Kicking the door closed once he stepped inside, I said, "Say again?"

"I feel like I should be apologizing but I don't know what for. They're what the florist called 'I screwed up somehow' flowers. Apparently, a big seller there." He looked apologetic; his eyes were sad, and his normally bright façade lacked its spark. Even his dreads seemed dismal.

"You don't need to apologize." But I took the flowers into the kitchen, inhaling the fragrant scent of three roses.

"I do." He stood at the entrance to my galley kitchen, lips sealed until after I'd placed the flowers into a vase and set the bouquet on the tiny table. "I want to talk to you."

My heart skipped a beat, but I allowed him to hold my hand and drag me into the living room. I sat beside him on the hand-me-down sofa, twisting in my spot to face him.

"I'm sorry about this morning."

I wasn't going to talk, I wanted him to spill without input or prodding from me. His thoughts had to be his own. Maybe he'd be more honest that way and say what he meant, and not what I hoped to hear. But I didn't know what I wanted to hear.

"When you said those words this morning, it surprised me. I thought those words were only said in the throes of passion, not said casually over the breakfast table. And I realised in that moment, because of how you said it, that you meant it." His thumb rubbed the top of my knuckles. The bulge in his throat bobbed up and down as he swallowed. "I've never been told that."

"What? Like ever?" There was no way. Surely, Pamela or Marcus or Harry had said it. Every parent did. Hell, Sean and Randy must've told Scarlett a dozen times this morning alone and I was only there for an hour.

"Never ever." His gaze fell to the floor. "Like I said last night, my parents weren't great parents."

"Oh, Korey." My heart broke a little more for him and his lack of lovable upbringing. It was a wonder he was as kind and sensitive as he was.

A sharp inhale of air bordered on the angry side, but as I gazed at him, he was anything but. "I don't need your pity, I just wanted to let you know that it surprised me. I didn't know how to act, or what to say."

"Did you never have a girlfriend tell you that?"

"I was never in a relationship long enough to find out."

"What about that one who pulled the 'I'm late' on you?"

"There was no love."

Oh wow. I swallowed and reached for his hand, giving him a sweet squeeze.

"Until I met you, I wasn't sure about a lot of things, but mostly about love. I didn't know if I could ever be loved, or if I was even lovable."

The tears welled up in my eyes. How awful it must be to go through life shouldering that. I inched closer to him.

"When you left, I felt something inside me start to ache. I wasn't sure what it was, but it really hurt. Here." He placed a free hand over his chest. "And it scared me."

"I wasn't leaving you." I gave his knee a rub stunned that he was so insecure about us, if you could call it insecure. "I was just upset over your response and needed to think. But if it helps, it scared me too." I wiped away a fallen tear. "I've never felt this way about someone."

He took a long finger and traced a wet path on my cheeks. "And I'm sorry I didn't understand. Love is such a foreign thing for me, but that ache spoke volumes and it finally clicked inside me. I love you too."

The words melted my heart, erasing all the negative feelings I'd been holding onto.

"I want to do better by you. So I made a phone call after you left and after I realised what was happening inside my head and heart. I'm expecting a call from Marcus soon."

I frowned and gave my head a quick shake. "What? Why?"

"I asked him for a job. Maybe it's time I did something more important with my life."

My swallow was loud and clear, and I was sure he heard it too. "What about your lease and the constant adventures?"

"That depends on Marcus. If he can hook me up with a job here, then I'll sign and stay. If not, then I'll go."

The inside of my cheek pinched against my teeth. "What would that mean for us? If your job isn't here?" I wasn't sure I wanted to know.

"I hope you'll come with me." His eyes held desire and confidence.

And leave my family behind? Leave my friends? What about my jobs? And college? I was meeting with my advisor this week to narrow my choice. I'd been accepted for a September admission and I'd already put it off when Ben screwed me out of my money.

My head started to swirl as I thought about the possibility of a future with him. Was it too fast to think about maybe moving away with him? We were a fresh couple. Still young.

An ache formed in my chest, but I wasn't sure if it was a warning or not.

Korey twirled a random design atop my knee that I couldn't figure out. "I don't know yet, so don't start panicking. Let's get the logistics sorted out first."

Okay. I could wait. And hope that the job would be here, because everything else in my life was. "But if the job isn't here, why not stay waiting tables? You make decent money and great tips."

"It's not a lifestyle, and certainly not a career. My lease expires at the end of next month on May 30th, and if I'm staying, it's time to man up and do the right thing."

He was man enough for me, changing his income level wouldn't change anything between us. "I'm okay with working with you. We've been doing well with it so far."

"For now. What happens when I'm promoted to manager?"

I raised my eyebrow at him. As if.

"What? Niall said he's considering it. It doesn't take much to become a manager of a small establishment like Westside."

"Oh." My mind went blank. It could be a huge loss to the company to have him switch roles from jovial server to huffy manager. Customers came and lined up to sit in his section, I doubted someone like Evanora had the same. I certainly didn't.

His finger hooked my chin and tipped it up, his dark eyes searched mine. "Whatever happens, I love you, Shayne."

"And I love you." Not fully believing his 'adventure' days were over.

When Korey's cell rang a couple of hours later, I knew

who it was before he answered. He pulled out of our comfortable, sexless embrace and reached for the phone on the coffee table

"Marcus," he said, putting the phone to his ear. "What's the word? And what did he say? Really. Okay. Starting when? Six weeks, eh? That's pretty damn perfect."

He smiled in my direction. Maybe it was something local. My heart pounded a little with the excitement.

"Well, thanks. I appreciate that. Oh yeah when? Maybe. Give me a call closer to, and we can work something out." He tossed the phone onto the edge of the couch.

The longer he sat there speechless, the faster my blood pulsed. Finally, I couldn't take it anymore. His expression was blank, and I wasn't sure if that was a good thing or a bad thing. "So? What did he say?"

"Well, lady luck is on my side. Our side." A bigger smile had never been smiled but he stood there with his feet shoulder width apart, his arms swaying back and forth. "There's a maternity position coming up in six weeks. What he can do is shuffle a few higher levelled employees around, and I can get a very entry level job after that."

"Okay." My butt wiggled to the edge of the couch. An entry level position was great.

"But it's in Lethbridge."

Wow. "That's like eight hours from here." I pushed back and curled up on my side of the couch, my arms wrapping tightly around my legs.

"And it's a fantastic opportunity."

My voice fell into the pit of sourness. "Why there? There was nothing here?"

"No. He operates a few branches. This was the best he could do."

"But it's Lethbridge." So far away. I could entertain the thought of Calgary maybe, and then my family was still only a three-hour drive away. Heading to the bottom of the province eliminated an overnight visit. If I went it would be a weekend visit at minimum, especially if I drove up.

"We're in a recession." He reached for my hand and pulled me onto my feet. "Plus, we can have a new adventure together. You can truly break away from your family and carve out your own future."

Break away from my family? "But I don't know what I want from it."

"All that matters is that we're together, right?"

I nodded slowly. "We can do that here. I don't understand why you'd have to relocate."

"Because I can get a real job."

My fist hit the edge of the sofa. "You can do that here. Or stay in your serving job." I hated that I sounded whiny, but I wasn't ready to pack up and move eight hours away from all that I grew up with.

"You don't understand."

I pushed him back. "I really don't. And I'm trying hard to."

"We're young, and our entire future lays ahead of us, uncharted and ready for discovery. I've seen all I want of Edmonton, and if I'm going to lock myself into something more permanent, I don't know that I want to do it here. I'm not in love with this city."

"What? How can you not love it here? It's beautiful." My hands waved through the air as I pointed in all directions.

"The mountains are four hours away, there's no decent lake nearby."

Well, there was a few, but yeah, decent? Maybe not. I don't know that I'd swim in them.

He nearly spit out his words. "It's disgustingly cold here in the winter."

That part was true. When the worst of it hit, it was quite unbearable. And those were the days when you wish you didn't need to leave the warmth of your house. Car probably wouldn't start anyway.

"Think about it. It's not permanent, we could sign a year's lease and I can keep my eyes open for a position back here or we can find something else."

"What would I do for a job?" I was sure there were boat loads of server positions, and maybe even nanny jobs too. They're a dime a dozen, but I hadn't ever considered either of those a career choice. They were temporary to pay off the bills accumulated in Ben's wake. And to prepare for my future. I was intrigued by the birth attendant thing, but I needed to look into that more, but as it was, I was enrolled at Grant Mac in the fall. Ready to start *my* adventure. My college adventure.

I wasn't sure I wanted to give it up by moving so far away. From my friends. From my family. From my niece. What would I do for connections? How would I meet and befriend perfect strangers? I looked up into Korey's face. Mixing work and pleasure could end up taking me miles away from all that I loved and held dear.

"I need time to think about it, but I honestly think you need to reconsider moving, or if you're concerned about your lease, move in here with me." It's not like he had a lot of stuff, and shouldn't that be the next logical step in a relationship rather that packed up and setting sail far away? "That could work. We could totally make it work." I hated the plea sound in my voice, but I suddenly felt desperate.

His hand grazed over my belly. "I promise to think on it, if you do."

Hmm. I supposed I could *think* on it but based on the panic taking root deep in my soul, my answer would be no.

Chapter Seventeen

I hung outside on the picnic table near the back door of Westside, waiting for Jasper to finish up with Niall. After our shift, he wanted to give his two-week notice, although it was closer to three weeks now. He'd already given notice at his apartment, refusing to renew his lease. I'd hoped I'd be able to change his mind and at least have him move in with me. So far, all that had happened was a variety of disagreements.

My heart skipped a beat when the two men emerged out into the open air. I stopped picking at my nails and watched as they stepped over to the table.

Niall extended his hand. "I'm sure going to miss you. You were a valuable team member." With his other hand, he gave Jasper's shoulder a squeeze.

"Time to move on to a new adventure." Jasper smiled in my direction. He kept pushing that my adventure didn't have to be at Grant Mac in the fall, it could be with him in Lethbridge. "But it's been a slice."

Niall removed a package of cigarettes from his pocket and waved them around. "Anyone mind?"

I did, but kept my mouth shut. We were outside, and he was downwind of me. Instead of speaking my mind, I shook my head and resumed pushing back my cuticles with my longest fingernail.

Niall smoked his cigarette and, in between drags,

mumbled about the hockey playoffs.

For the most part, I tuned them out. All my thoughts revolved around the future and around my boyfriend and whether they could exist together. When we first started hooking up, it was only supposed to be for fun. That had been my plan. I didn't want to be tied down. Wanted to start my adventure in college, within the safe confines of family and all that I knew.

A tepid adventure, as Korey called it. One that came with all sorts of safety nets. A true adventure was breaking free of everything familiar and trusting that all would be fine in a new location. He'd been doing it his whole adult life.

But somewhere over the past three months, my heart had changed. I'd fallen for him. Hard and fast. And I hadn't meant for that to happen.

"Hey, Earth to Shayne."

Hearing my real name, snapped me out of my head and I looked for the source of the voice. Korey.

"See you both tomorrow." Niall extinguished his stub and dropped it into the can of sand at the base of the table. "Don't be so chatty next time, Jade." He waved and walked back into the restaurant.

"Tired?" Korey asked.

I slowly shook my head. "No, just a lot on my mind." My gaze flitted to the door and back. "You really gave your notice?"

"I sure did."

"No regrets?"

"None. I'm looking forward to the change. It's good for the soul."

"Are you tired? I mean figuratively, like tired of me, and tired of what's going on between us. So tired that you're willing to up and move without much thought about it."

He sighed, the same soul-shattering sigh I got whenever it was brought up, which had been daily lately.

"Let's continue this back at my place. Or would yours be better?"

I didn't know what I wanted. It sucked. I shrugged. "I don't care."

"Yeah, you do. Let's go to your place." He nudged my foot with his. "C'mon." He rose and took my hand. "I'm not leaving without you."

Does that mean if I stay, in Edmonton, you will too? But I knew that's not what he meant. It was after eleven on a Friday night, and he wasn't going to leave me alone sitting at a picnic table in a less than desirable neighbourhood.

I wrapped my fingers through his and followed him over to his car.

The ride was as silent as ever. Not even the radio played. Just the kind of quiet silence that comes with the windows down and the engine revving as he worked to be the first off the line. But no words were spoken.

With my apartment door locked and chain slid into place, I headed into my bedroom to change. A minute later I walked into the living room and curled up under the blanket on my couch.

"I've let you stay in your head for the trip home, but I want you to tell me what's on your mind. They only way we're going to make this work is if we communicate. And you've totally shut down."

"I know."

"So, let's continue what you started back at Westside."

I sighed and pulled my legs to my chest, resting my chin on top. "Are you tired of me?"

A pained smile spread across his face. "Never."

"Then why the desire to leave. I don't understand."

"Shayne, I love you. I want to do right by you, and that means getting a real job and making a career out of it, to eventually support you. I can't do that on a server's salary."

"But you can get a real job here. This isn't no hick town, there's over a million people living here. Real jobs are everywhere."

He sunk into his side of the couch. "And with my level of

education, do you think I'll be able to get a job in a real job?" He air-quoted real job. "There are people graduating from university with degrees who aren't getting a 'real job' and are working at a variety of retail and restaurant jobs. Those people have the education. Are you hearing me, Shayne? They have the qualifications and I don't, and they're not working in their fields. And if they can't get a 'real job', how in the hell will I?" He rubbed the whiskers on his chin. "Marcus bent over backward to get me into the bank. A place where I can learn as I go, and maybe, move up the ranks. But that gift means I need to move to Lethbridge."

"But you don't need a real job. I didn't fall in love with you because you were working on climbing some corporate ladder, I fell in love with you because of your infectious nature, your charm and the way you make me feel. You could work at Westside for the rest of your life, and as long as we're together, I'd be happy." And together here would be the icing on the cake.

A grim expression filled his face. "I don't buy that. And you deserve better than that."

"Why do I do deserve better?"

"Because someday, we'll get married, and eventually we'll have children. And I'll need a much better job for those things."

A loud gasp escaped me as a cold sensation settled in me. Those things were so far off in the future, and I'd never entertained them. Marriage, kids? Not right now, thank you very much. God, I'm nineteen-years-old.

"You've never considered it?"

My eyes went wide. "Never." My words caused him to pull back. "You have?"

"Not in much detail, but yes, I've thought about it."

"Isn't it too fast?"

"Not if you know it's right." He inched a little closer to me. "It feels right to me. I've never been so sure of a relationship in my life. And this, this I believe in. Don't you believe in us?"

That I didn't have the answer to. I had no idea. I loved him for sure, there was no question about that.

"It's like you said in the hospital, it's not like we're going to run out and procreate right now. We have years ahead of us for that. But I see you in my future. And marriage, that can come years down the line."

I started shivering.

"Shayne, I'm not saying this to scare you."

"Well, it's not working. I'm terrified." I huddled deeper under the blanket and stared up at Korey.

"Of what?"

It was hard to put my finger on exactly. "I need to think."

"Is it the moving away?"

"Partly." Mostly.

"It's only scary because you've never done it. When you moved out of your parent's house, what did you feel?"

That was a while back, not long after I graduated. I thought back to that summer day. "I was excited, mostly. Ready to tackle the world, be own my own and make adult decisions. But it was also a little scary. I had to make sure I had the funds to pay my bills each month and put food on the table. I needed to learn how to take care of things on my own."

He smiled. "Exactly. But you were excited. Those were the first words to come out of your mouth. And you did it. Even when that ex-boyfriend took your money, you still made it work."

"Randy helped me out that first month. I wasn't completely on my own."

"My point is that you didn't pack it in and move back home. You found a way to deal with it. Like a grown up."

Slowly, I was starting to see things the way he did. Every six months or a year, as it was this time, Korey packed up and moved. Because he knew he'd be alright. He could manage on his own. He maybe even had a safety net, even if he didn't believe it. I was sure Marcus would welcome him home if he ever felt like he needed help. He did get him a job, so there was a safety net there.

"And?" I sensed that they way he sat on the edge of the sofa, inching his way closer to me, that he had more to tell me.

There was a sparkle in his eyes that held a tiny morsel of hope. "But what about college?"

"Can't you take your courses online? I'm sure your base courses would allow it."

I'd never thought about it. Maybe that was a possibility.

A pleading look surfaced on his face and he held my hands. "Look at places with me. In Lethbridge. We can sign a six-month lease, and if you're really homesick, we can come back here. I can check within the bank to watch for positions to open here, if you don't fall in love with the adventure there. It's six months. It would be you and me. And we're young. This is our time to do this. You can do this when you have a family, and when you're older, you don't have the energy to move around. We can do that now."

"But my family?"

"It's six months. And you can visit. They can visit. You're not cut off from them, I promise, I wouldn't do that to you. You can Skype or Facetime daily."

Six months was more appealing than a year, that's for sure. One hundred and eighty days. But I'd never been away from my family for longer than a week, could I make it work? I wouldn't be alone, I'd have Korey.

I still wasn't 100% convinced but I slowly found myself leaning toward the idea of at least looking at available apartments. In Lethbridge.

Chapter Eighteen

I sat in Lily's kitchen while Jordan was playing with Mary in the living room, steps away from where I was. A full mug of hot chocolate warmed my hands.

The rain danced off the deck railing beyond the open window, its freshness rolling in with each gust of wind. It was a blustery day and rather than meet at the playpark where we figured everyone else would also be, we changed locations to her house.

She set down a batch of homemade cookies. "Tell me about this new place?"

I tried to put the excitement in my voice. If I played the part, surely I would start to truly feel it and believe in it as I wasn't fully on board yet. "It's this tiny but beautiful one bedroom, on the top floor of a giant walk-up. It's within walking distance to the university and the rec centre. The rent's a little high but with the two of us paying half, it's actually cheaper than what we each pay now."

"He signed the lease, did he?" She pushed her dark hair off her face, the bags under her eyes darker and fuller than I'd ever seen before.

"Yes."

"And you're going with him?"

My heart dropped into my gut, and the sourness built. "Yes." It was the hardest decision I'd ever made, but in the end, I could only blame my youth if it didn't work out.

"What changed your mind? You seemed like you were wavering a bit."

"It's hard to explain."

She scoffed. "So, let me guess, you're in love." She drawled out the last word, giving it a negative connotation.

I narrowed my eyes slightly. "It's more than that." But how to explain? My sister had moved three hours away, for four years, and she did fine. Sean also went away for a spell for school, and he moved back. He'd been fine too. So why couldn't I? After all, like Korey repeated over and over, it wasn't permanent and who knew? Maybe I could fall in love with a city that didn't get so blustery cold.

A 'real job', something like Korey had waiting for him at the bank, wasn't as high up on my list just yet. I was sure I could find lots of ladies who wanted to give birth and let me help them as with a little research, I'd found a doula course to attend my second weekend there.

But I was still nervous. Something wasn't sitting quite right and I couldn't figure it out. It frustrated me to no end.

"How did your family take it?"

"Better than I did at telling them." I'd been a nervous wreck and paced a little too much to pretend nothing was bothering me. But I felt it was my time to share, after all, we'd be packing up and leaving. In just under a month. "Dina thought it was great and went on and on about how I'd love my freedom. Sean was happy, but Randy held back a little."

Too much sadness had crept across his face. It had been difficult, and Randy took it the hardest. He kept his distance and cradled Scarlett, who had legally become theirs six days prior to my major announcement.

While I put on a brave face, I swallowed my fear and shared with my family the details about how I was going to make it work, the cute apartment Korey and I were renting and the great new job his sort of step-dad got him. Figuring it was best, I decided not to explain his whole family situation, especially since my parents were so enthused I'd found *the one*. They claimed I had a good head on my shoulders as with the upcoming course I wasn't dependant on Korey financially. They did express displeasure in my temporary postponement of college for another year but reminded me it would be there when I came home.

If I came home.

If I went at all.

Although my body was on board, my mind hadn't been convinced yet. I sure hoped it got there before moving day.

A loud bang startled me out of my thoughts, and I whipped my head around to Mary. She smacked the fireplace mantle with a plastic toy baseball bat.

Lily ignored it all. "Wow. I'm so jealous."

"For real?" I couldn't fathom the reason why. There was zero about me that anyone could be jealous of.

Mary banged again, harder, and the bat snapped.

Jordan looked to me and I lifted myself out of my chair, ready to go get involved. But Mary didn't act like she cared that the bat was broken. Nor did Lily. She hadn't even turned around when it busted.

Lily grabbed my hand and pulled me to her. "I'm leaving Jason."

My eyes bugged out of my head. "What?" I tried to keep my voice low so as to not disturb the children. A tremor shook through me. "When?" My voice was barely above a whisper.

"I'm not sure yet. But soon."

"Have you talked to Jason?" I pleaded as best as I could.

She released her hold on me and lowered her head. "Multiple times. He says it's just a rough patch and we'll get through it, maybe we need therapy, or a maid or something."

"So, take him up on those." I certainly would if I were in her shoes.

"I would if that were the issue. But I'm tired of this. I'm tired of being in a loveless marriage and being a mother. I never wanted all this." She waved her hand around. "And there's no escape. It's endless. Day in, day out. Same thing over and over. It's mediocre at best."

I couldn't believe my ears. "So you're just going to up and leave?"

"Yep."

"What about the girls?"

"I haven't figured that out yet."

My blood rushed so strongly, it drowned out my thoughts and my grip tightened around my mug, turning my knuckles white. I glanced around the living room, eyeing Jordan as he walked away from Mary and settled on the floor to play with the trains.

What was Lily thinking? She was crazy, and something in her had snapped. That much was clear. Who could just abandon their family and be so blasé about it?

"You have no game plan at all?" I fished for more information. I figured I'd gather what I could and formulate my own plan to help her. Get her a night in a hotel so she could have a break. Maybe I should take her out and get her some pampering. Or, better thought, maybe I should call her family? Did she have other family? Thinking back, she never mentioned any. No siblings. No parents. "What about your family?"

"You think they'd care?"

"The girls will. They'd miss you like crazy."

"They're young. They'd get over it." Her eyes drifted away to lands I'd never know. "I can't do it anymore. They're breaking me." Her tears fell.

"Lily," I took her hand. "How can I help you? What can I do to make things better for you? You say the word and I'll bust my butt to make it happen. Tell me."

She shook her head. "There's nothing you can do."

I pulled my kitchen chair close to her and sat on it, right on the edge. "There has to be. Take a week and stay with me at the apartment. We can make it a girl's week."

She pushed her mug with enough force it caught in the gap where you insert a table leaf and spilled. "Everything would just be waiting for me here at the end of it. Like this. You think anyone other than me is going to clean that up?" A timer went off on her phone. "Ten minutes until Myrah gets home from preschool." Tears streamed down her face.

"Do you need to go?" I wasn't about to leave her, I sensed too much unpredictability from her, but I'd sure as heck follow her.

"No. Her bus drops her off at the corner. I just need to meet her there." She rose and swiped a hand across her face. "Want more to drink?" She left the little mess of spilled coffee on the table.

I stared at my hot chocolate. It was still over half full. "I'm good." With the napkin under my mug, I dabbed at the spilled coffee.

She whispered under her breath. "I know you are."

I watched her as she paced around the kitchen, pulling a basket of berries from the fridge along with a package of cheese. Aimlessly, like a robot, she cored and sliced the strawberries.

The alarm went off again.

"I need to go meet Myrah at the corner. Just wait here, and keep an eye on Mary, will you?"

"Of course." My focus never left Lily, but I supposed it needed to.

She rubbed her eyes and pinched her cheeks and bent over to check her reflection on the stainless-steel toaster. "I don't look like I've been crying, do I?"

Truth or lie? "Sort of."

"Oh well." She headed for the front of her house and the screen door banged shut.

The kids started fighting over a train, and I walked over to intervene.

Mary, the spitting image of her mother, held a red engine in her hands.

"Mine," Jordan wailed and pushed Mary into the couch.

Mary threw the train at him, which bounced off his

forehead, leaving an angry red mark.

I grabbed the little engine and placed it atop the fireplace. "Now neither of you get to play with it." I searched around and found two different trains of the same colour and passed them out. "Here."

Kids were so resilient. Each took their new item and drove it along the edge of the ottoman, the red train long since abandoned, their spat behind them.

A harsh bang on the screen door, and a creaking as it opened. Another followed when it slammed shut. Walking towards it, I spotted Myrah dumping her wet backpack and coat at the door. I waited for Lily to appear.

"Myrah, where's your mom?" Panic rose in my voice as the little hairs at the back of my head stood at attention.

"Dun know." She shrugged. Puddles marked her path as she left the front door and sauntered into the living room; her wet boots still on.

I glanced between her and the door, bile rising fast in my stomach. "Doesn't she meet you at the corner?"

She gave me a bizarre look, her head cocking to the side. "No. I just come in."

"Excuse me." I bolted to the door and down the front steps to the edge of the driveway, my head frantically flipping left and right. No one was outside. Not a bus. Not a child. And not a mother waiting for her daughter to get off a bus.

I surveyed the driveway, wiping my dripping hair off my eyes. Her car was still there. Where did she go? She just walked outside not three minutes ago. Rain thundered around me, soaking through my t-shirt and jeans. There's no way she just vanished. It was impossible.

I walked back up the stairs and into the house, closing the screen door behind me but scanning and watching, hoping she'd pop back into the house. "Myrah," I called out as I dripped onto the floor. "Can you grab me a towel please?"

She dragged one from the bathroom.

"Was your mommy out there?"

"I didn't see her. Are you babysitting me today?" There was a perkiness in her question.

Wiping myself down, I marched into the kitchen. Lily's phone still sat on the island, beside the plate of diced strawberries. Something in the pit of my stomach said she'd left and wasn't coming back. Just like that.

I grabbed her phone and flipped through her contacts. "C'mon, Jason, pick up." But he didn't. Using my cell phone, I dialled his number. After the third attempt, he finally answered. "Jason, it's Shayne, Lily's friend. Can you come home? It's an emergency – Lily just disappeared."

Chapter Nineteen

Lily up and walked away, leaving behind questions, upset children, a worried husband and frantic friends. Jason came home immediately, and after the required 24-hour wait with the police, because she could be just out shopping and needing a break, she was declared a missing person. Nothing in her bedroom was gone. Their bank account had not been touched either and no one had heard from her. We were no closer to answers than we were the moment she stepped out the front door.

Between the cops, Jason and my family, I'd retold my conversation with Lily so many times over, it drained me. Nothing made sense. She'd simply vanished.

"Where could she be?" I asked Korey constantly, like he knew and was waiting for me to ask in the right pleading voice before he'd answer.

"I don't have the answers you're looking for. Only she does." He sighed and uncurled the fist I made. Lately, my hands preferred the tightness.

"Pamela did this, right? She up and abandoned you." As if that helped, trudging up a memory of his adoptive mother leaving him.

"Yep."

"And did you ever find her?"

His voice was even, but devoid of emotion. "Nope. I

swear I saw her once, but I never pursued it. I didn't care. She'd left me. I wasn't about to run after her and beg for forgiveness."

I sighed, as had become custom. "Will the girls be like that?"

He shrugged and pulled me closer. "I don't know. Maybe. Maybe she'll come back. Maybe she's better than Pamela."

"It's been three weeks. Wouldn't she have returned by now?" Too many unanswered questions. I buried my nose in the crook of his neck.

He ran his hand up and down my spine. "Why don't you just rest? You've been going full throttle for weeks now." He kissed my forehead.

Rest? What was that?

In order to maintain my sanity, I had tried to maintain a normal routine in my life, but it was difficult at best. That horrid first week, I'd wake and get Jordan, taking him to Lily's house where I'd help Jason and the girls. He had taken time off work but used that time to pursue every last possibility of hope. While he hunted and dared to dream he'd find her, I tried to keep the girls as routine as possible. Off to school Maggie and Myrah'd go, and Mary and Jordan would play and laugh, although it felt so weird to babysit in her home, as I kept checking the doors waiting for Lily to waltz in like nothing happened.

After I dropped Jordan off with Aimee at three, I headed over to Westside and faked my way through another shift, wondering if each customer that breezed through the doors could be her. I kept hoping she'd just show up, if for no other reason than to say she was okay. I felt like I was slowly losing my mind.

Between Westside and Jordan, I only had a week left before the big move, and I had yet to pack; too exhausted after working fifteen-hour days to do much else other than crawl under the blankets and pray to a god I didn't believe in, asking Him to watch over Lily and keep her safe.

I picked up my silent phone again, willing her name to show on the display.

"Give it here," Korey asked, his hand out.

I let it fall into his palm.

"If anyone calls, I'll be sure to let you know, but you need to stop looking at it."

"But–"

"No buts, Shayne. I know it's hard to accept, but she's gone. She's not coming back. They. Never. Come. Back. You worrying about it, isn't good for your health."

I hated that he was right, but still, I was going to worry. And looking, or not looking at my phone wasn't going to stop me. Rolling over, I put both feet on the floor.

"Where are you going?"

"I should pack."

"Jesus Christ, it's midnight."

I glanced at the clock. Seriously, hours disappeared out of my day like… disappeared… I couldn't even finish the thought. My head fell into my hands. "I can't ... do this anymore."

The mattress moved as he scrambled to sit beside me, a warm arm draping across my shoulders. I turned to face him, but rather than look at him, I kept my face hidden under my hands.

"Shayne, you haven't slept properly in three weeks. You're working like a dog, trying to be everything to everybody. You need a break." Under his breath, I heard, "Lethbridge will be so good for you."

I started sobbing. Tears I hadn't let loose because I was supposed to be calm and positive when around Jason or the girls, or because I was at work and you leave your problems at the door. Or maybe it was because everything around me felt like it was moving too fast. Between the missing friend and the relocation, I wasn't sure what to do anymore. Tears of sadness, confusion, and hurt fell from me like a waterfall.

Korey wrapped his arms tighter around me. He said nothing, just held me together to prevent me from falling apart.

It was after noon when I woke up. The air in the bedroom was stifling and I'd been sweating as the lone sheet on the bed was damp. Grabbing it, I wrapped it around myself and stumbled over to the window to crank it open and allow some freshness in. I savoured that sweet smell, the scent of summer heat, a warning of the warmth rolling in.

Since we weren't at his place doing naked Saturdays, I jumped into a pair of shorts and a tank top and made my way to the living room.

Korey typed away feverishly on his laptop, a newly purchased item to help prep him for his upcoming job. When he wasn't consoling me, or working at Westside, he was partaking in every banking webinar Marcus sent him links for. "I'm still a one finger typer," he said, glancing up from the keyboard.

I sat beside him and placed my head on his shoulder. It moved beneath me quite a bit, so I held it back up. "It'll come with time and practice." I watched as he scrolled through dozens of pages on one site. "Why didn't you wake me up?"

"Are you kidding?" He looked me deep in the eye. "You needed your sleep. Besides, a bomb could've gone off and you wouldn't have woken." He brushed a strand of hair behind the arm of my glasses. "How did you sleep?"

"Like a log." Not the best sleep I'd ever had, but I slept solidly. My body didn't ache like it had over the last few days, and I felt more in control of my feelings and emotions. "Thank you for last night. For letting me…" I shuddered. "Let it out."

"No worries." He closed the lid on his laptop and sauntered into the kitchen. Baggy sweats hung off his hips, but not in an attractive way. They were so old and ratty, they had to be Marcus's from when he was a teen.

I blinked away my sour expression and met him in the kitchen. "Everything okay?"

"Yeah." He helped himself to a cup of coffee. The pot was already halfway done, so he'd been up for some time. My phone came sliding across the counter top in my direction.

"Jason's called three times already."

"What?" I listened to my messages. Each one said the same thing, to call when I can as he wondered if I could help today. I sighed and put the phone down on the counter. Perhaps there was some truth to what Lily said, and that Jason was wholly negligent on what a parent needed to do.

"Everything okay on the home front?" His tone held a hint of nastiness.

I shrugged. "He wants me to call when I can."

"So, call him back."

"I don't want to right now." I grabbed myself a mug and inhaled the strong aroma while I poured. I'd shouldered so much over the past few weeks, may as well drink the adult crap that goes with it. "I want a few hours where it's not me chasing after the girls, or running after Jordan, or fetching a customer's order. I want you. To get lost with, in you, even if it's only for an hour. I just need the escape." I scanned around the kitchen. "Then I need to start packing. This could take me longer than I think."

"Well, if it's escape you want, I can provide assistance." He removed the mug from my hand, replacing it with his hand, and wrapped his fingers through mine.

"I was hoping you'd say that." For the first time in a while, I smiled.

His lips brushed against mine, tender and soft. Long strokes from his hand grazed up and down my back, sending shivers of a positive nature rippling out to my extremities. He released my hand and caressed my cheek with it, akin to touching soft silk. The pads of his fingers trailed down and over my lips, heating me up from the inside out.

His excitement pressed into me like a stone, hard against my hip, and I found myself begging for him. To feel his power as he takes me out of my head to other places where only instinctual senses are at play. To feel his hands all over my body, inch by inch, making my skin come alive with electricity.

I need this. I want this.

I wrapped my fingers carefully through his dreads, and pulled his head closer, thrusting my tongue deep into his mouth. The moan deep within his chest rattled against mine. Throaty, it was a huge turn on. Like a volcano, the heat built in my core, spread to the top, and threatened to explode before we're ready.

"Let's go to the bedroom," I breathed out in rasps as his kisses left a trail of sweetness along my collarbone, and over onto my shoulder. I never knew shoulders could be erotic, but Korey seemed to know every little place that would fire up my synapses and have me begging for more.

He ignored my desire for a more comfortable space, instead his hands slipped my tank top off, baring my breasts to the outside world. Thank goodness my kitchen window looked out into a cloudless void, and I'd care more about the building perpendicular to mine if he wasn't cupping my breasts and making my nipples stand at attention. Reaching into the freezer, he retrieved an ice cube, and I stared in rapt attention as he dangled it above me.

The icy water dripped down, sizzling against my skin, and he lapped it up. Slowly, he drew a circle around my peaks, moving towards the centre. My highly charged skin raised goosebumps which he counteracted with the heat of his tongue. The contrast in temperatures was riveting and I closed my eyes to savour all the sensations.

A knock sounded on my apartment door which was only a few feet from the counter Korey had me pressed against.

"What the hell?" I jerked my head and stared at Korey.

Although no one opened the door, he covered me with his chest, pulling me close. He whispered because the door was thin enough to let all sound through. "Who'd be here?"

"Beats me." But I continued to stare at the door. "Oh my god, what if it's Lily?" I pushed him out of the way and pulled my tank top back on. Stopping at the peephole, I peered out. "Oh, it's Dina."

"I heard that," she said beyond the door.

So much for an escape. I looked back at Korey who glared as he walked past me toward the bedroom hiding his pleasure. I yanked open the door. "What do you want?"

She stood there, a pile of boxes at her feet and a packed tote bag hanging off her shoulder. "You told me to come for twelve-thirty."

"I did?" I blinked a few times and shook my head. "When?"

"Thursday. You begged me to come help." She kicked the boxes in and leaned them against the front closet. "You work at four today, right?"

Do I? I didn't know, maybe. I didn't even remember asking her for help, so perhaps I was wrong about my work schedule too.

"Oh, don't look so confused." Her heavy tote slid off her shoulder and landed with a thump at her feet.

"When did I ask you on Thursday?"

"I don't know. Daytime? Check your texts."

Turning my back to her, I strutted into the kitchen and located my phone. I thumbed through my messages and read hers.

"See." Her voice came from over my shoulder.

Wow, I must've been tired when I sent that as I was usually mentally organized enough to remember things like this. I rested against the countertop. "Well, since you're here and I invited you…" I glanced toward the bedroom wondering if Korey had made himself decent for Dina's sake.

"Korey here?" Dina held up a coffee cup.

"Um… yes."

"Right here," he said. Dressed in something a little newer, and certainly cleaner, he walked into the galley kitchen, gently pushing past Dina. "That's mine." He reached for his mug and held it in his hands.

Dina poured herself a cup of coffee and faced Korey. "You excited about the new job? You start in what, two weeks?"

"Sixteen days. We travel down next Monday, giving us a

week to settle in before I try to be an adult. I'm not un-excited about that."

Dina turned to me. "What's that even mean?"

I shrugged. "I don't know."

"Xander speaks the same way." She threw her hands in the air. "Guys."

"It'll be fine." Korey eyed us both, until his gaze drifted towards the door. "Well I can see Dina has some big plans, which I'm sad to tell you, won't include me. I should finish up this webinar so I'm heading home." He grabbed his laptop and stood at the door. "See you at work." A tender kiss fell upon my lips.

I wanted it to be so much more but given that my sister stood ten feet behind me and was burning a hole in the back of my head, I bid him adieu.

"As always, Dina, it's been a slice."

I closed the door and crossed my arms over my chest. "So, where to begin?"

# # #

Dina stood beside me, sighing as she wrapped the small stack of plates in a dishtowel and placed it inside the box. On her notepad she scratched down the contents and sealed it up with packing tape, affixing a sticky note to the outside. "Don't remove until it's numbered." She shook her finger at me as if I'd forget the scolding I'd received less than an hour ago.

"How'd you do it?" It had been on my mind for a while, and I didn't want to hold it in anymore.

"Well, I take inventory of what we packed and later, I'll make a spreadsheet–"

"Not this." I waved to the three boxes sitting on the kitchen counter. "The moving away part."

"Oh." She spun to face me. "That." She inhaled sharply and released it in a huff. "It wasn't hard. But then, I'd been living at home so it was easy to leave behind the invasion of privacy for the comfort of my own place."

"Yeah." I'd been on my own almost since the day I graduated high school. Where as I couldn't wait to branch out on my own, everyone had been near me and I never felt isolated. I wasn't trying to escape the way Dina did, or Sean. Being near my family was a priority to me.

"You'll get used to it." She patted my shoulder as if I were a child.

"To what?"

"Learning to fend for yourself."

"I do that now."

"Sort of, but it's different. If your car breaks down, you can't run to Daddy and bat your eyelashes and get it handled. It'll be good for you, and you'll grow up." Her condescending tone rattled me.

I never *batted my eyelashes* and got what I want. That was all her. Some people think the baby of the family gets spoiled but in truth, I had to fight harder to be heard. Dina was always Daddy's Girl, and Sean was Mommy's Boy. I was just me. If I wanted something, I did it on my own. What the hell was she talking about?

"Anyways, it's not so hard. And the distance is nice."

"You were only three hours away. I'm going to be eight."

"Even better."

"If it's so easy to be gone, why did you come back?" I raised my eyebrow at her, tired of her thinking this was going to be easy on me when it clearly had been hard on her.

"Xander."

"He was the *only* reason?" Why didn't I buy that theory?

"He was the only i*mportant* reason. He wanted to move here, and I was okay with that."

Because it's easier to fall and be close enough to have someone help you up than it is to do it alone. But I didn't say that to her. It would only start a fight, and I wasn't in the mood for that. I still had the living room to pack up. Dina's way was not a fast packing system, but she promised me the moving in would be a cinch. I had to trust in that because I'd helped her unpack and it *was* easier.

"What are you nervous about?"

I fiddled with the sharpie and drew my name on the box nearest me. "Who said I was nervous?"

"You're acting it." She closed the cupboard door and opened the one I stored food in. "What are you going to do with all of this?"

"I don't know." I hated to toss all of them, but the quizzical look on Dina's face told me she wasn't a fan of boxing up food. "Can't I move it?"

She sighed, a loud and frustrated sound. "Pass me that bin by the front door." Her pen scratched across the notebook. "I guess you can unpack this first." She opened the fridge. "Good gawd, are you packing all this?"

I shrugged. "Sure?"

"Do you have a cooler?"

"No."

"And this is why I need to help you with this. Does Korey have all these condiments? If so, will you really need two ketchups?"

I stared at the jars and plastic bottles, some more than half full. "I can't throw them out. It's so wasteful."

"I can."

"Dina, NO!" I said and grabbed the ketchup away from her.

"What's with you?"

"Just stop throwing my stuff away. You've tossed enough. Just because I *can* buy toilet paper in Lethbridge doesn't mean you need to throw out two perfectly good rolls. I can use them up or they can be extra padding in one of the boxes."

"But they are taking up necessary space."

"To you." I walked away and stood in my living room, surveying the untouched contents. Books, videos, games, furniture. So much left to pack. I honestly didn't think I had accumulated so much in my time on my own.

"Why don't you start by taking down this wall and putting the pictures into this." She handed me a shoebox. "They should all fit, right?"

I looked at my photo wall and nodded. It was borderline painful removing the pictures. So many memories stored in each smile or laugh or random pose. Would I hang these up at Korey's, I meant, our apartment? How would our decorating styles merge?

The first photo to come off and picked clean of the wall tac was a photo of Jordan and I. Would he miss me as much as I'd miss him? I wouldn't get to see him transition into a big brother and watch as he smooshed kisses onto his sibling. I wouldn't be there to play ball or read books to him. And as much as I knew that would be ending, there was the open possibility of visits. Aimee wouldn't have denied me that. But moving so far away? Any trip back here would surely be a busy one, would there be time to see him?

A few more photos came down off the wall, each one another memory. But pulling off the photo I had of the first time I held Scarlett caused an ache to form. If I was gone, I'd miss her year of firsts. It wouldn't be the same to watch her try her first taste of beans over facetime, or to see a picture of her first steps. If they needed a sitter, it wouldn't be—couldn't be—me. I wanted to be there. I wanted to see it all. I wanted to be a part of it all. I wanted to breathe her in and lavish in that new baby smell. She would probably grow out of that soon, and I'd miss it.

Dina poked her head around the wall. "Haven't you finished yet?" She stood with her hand on her hip. "You don't need to recall every single moment as you take it down." Her hand flew up and pulled off a few at a time.

"What are you doing?" I yelled and threw myself against the wall, interrupting her destruction. "Just stop. You nit-picking everything I'm doing or not doing isn't helping me."

"I'm trying to help."

"You're not." I brushed past her. "Just leave." I stormed

down the hall to my half-packed bedroom and slammed the door. A moment later another door slammed as I presumed Dina left.

I gave her a few minutes to make sure she didn't come back before I ventured out. Frustrated and tired, I didn't want to deal with her, or anyone for that matter. Padding into the kitchen, I surveyed the emptiness. Cupboard doors open, bareness staring me in the face.

What was I doing? Was I just rattled because everything seemed to be flipped upside down? Or was it more?

I slumped to the floor.

It was more. No matter what I said or did to try and convince myself, I wasn't ready. I didn't want to move.

How was I going to tell Korey?

Chapter Twenty

It didn't matter that I wasn't ready. I had given my notice at both my jobs, and with my apartment. I was jobless and homeless as of Monday morning. Problem was it wasn't what I wanted, and I was terrified to tell Korey. We'd spent many nights talking about and planning our futures in the new city, how could I walk away from that? How could I let him down?

I still didn't know how.

I sat outside on the porch watching Jordan and Lily's girls run through the sprinkler, hollering and screaming as only kids did. Jason, as had become customary, came home from work a little before three. It was my last day to help him out. Monday he was on his own as he had interviewed nannies as the day homes in the area were booked solid but the one he thought would work couldn't start until Tuesday.

He dropped into one of the lawn chairs beside me, after placing a package on the table. "For you."

"What? You didn't need to get me anything." I stared at the gift but didn't want to open it. It was another reminder that I was leaving.

"Go on, open it." He pushed it in my direction.

Caving, I tore open the envelope first and read the card as tears filled my eyes.

"I meant every word," he said. "I honestly don't know how I would've survived the past few weeks without you being here. I think you made this change in the family a little easier to cope with."

"Well, I don't know about that."

"Yeah. The girls are going to miss you." He focused his gaze on his girls. Myrah let out an ear-piercing scream as Maggi dumped a bucket of water over her. "And I'm going to miss you. You've been a rock for me."

"I'm happy to have been able to help. Well, not happy because it would be better…"

He stared at me with vacant eyes.

"You know what I mean." I felt my cheeks heat and in trying to distract myself from my own mouth, I reached for the gift bag. It was big and heavy. Tearing it open, I was surprised to see it was a pair of bookends. Made of wrought-iron, each side was a flower. A lily on one side, a rose on the other. It was exquisite. "Thank you."

"There's a book in there too."

I dug a little deeper and pulled it out. *A Little Book of Thank Yous.* Thumbing through, I backtracked to the first page when I spotted handwriting. Jason had inscribed it. *Thank yous are never enough. But you've left an imprint on us all, and I'm thankful for that gift.* More tears fell. "It's great. Thanks."

"For your new place. Figured this way, you'll never forget us."

"I wouldn't anyways." And it was true. We'd come a long way over the past few weeks, and he trusted me to take on a hard role of caring for his children. But I loved them all. And it hurt I had to say goodbye.

I was just about to grab Jordan and take him in to dry him off, when I spied Aimee out of the corner of my eye standing at the gate.

She waddled into the backyard after I waved her in. Aimee had started picking up Jordan from Jason's house not long after Lily's disappearance. Figured it was easier for her to go there and get Jordan than it was for me to drive to her house with the extra children, which I didn't like doing as I had to use Lily's van. There weren't enough seats in my car.

"Momma," Jordan called out when he spotted her. He ran over to give her a dripping wet hug.

"Hey, baby bear." She picked him up without batting an eye and straddled him on her hip. "This is for you." She handed me an envelope. "But open it later. Like after I'm gone." Her eyes filled up with tears.

I started fanning my own to keep them from getting too wet.

"Promise me when you're in town, you'll come for a visit."

"I promise."

She gave me a quick one-armed hug. "I hate goodbyes," she said, her voice cracking. Putting Jordan on his feet, they waved goodbye to Jason and the girls, and she headed to her car.

His bag. I ran inside and grabbed it, getting it to her car just before she drove off.

"For everything," she said and blew me a kiss after placing the bag on the passenger seat.

I waved and watched them drive away, hurt and emptiness filling my chest. "Two goodbyes down, only a dozen more to go." With a sigh, I headed back into the yard still clutching the envelope. Deciding it would be better to open it at home, I tucked it into the bag with Jason's gift.

"Well..." I said, standing and glancing around the yard.

Maggi threw a water balloon at Jason, and it landed at his feet, water spraying up and soaking him. But he laughed it off and chased her around the yard, her giggles the sweetest sound of joy.

I hoped they'd be okay. I hoped the nanny he hired was a perfect fit, one who can drive and shower them with all the love they'll need. Most of all, I kept hoping Lily would walk through the door, picking up after a restful break and rejoin her family. But a part of me hoped she doesn't. Because she didn't deserve to come back and fit right in like she'd never left. There's too much hurt to let it slide. I was confused by my feelings, and I hated myself for even thinking something like that. I was no better.

Hesitantly, I said goodbye to Jason, who graciously offered me the use of the in-law suite should I need a place to hang out when I come for a visit. And I made sure to say goodbye to each of the girls. I didn't want them to think all females in their lives left without a word. After a quick hug to each, I walked to my car. These were young relationships and they were tearing me apart. I'd only known Lily for less than two years, Jason even less.

How on earth was I going to say goodbye to my family?

I sat in my car and stared at the brick building Westside was housed in. Old and weathered down, it had served as a turning point in my life. It helped me pay off my bills, it taught me what it was like to be on the serving side of a restaurant, and most importantly, there I'd found love. And that was the hardest thing to walk away from, but I was 99% sure, I'd never make it so far away from my family. I was too tethered to them. Wiping my face, I headed to work my last shift at Westside.

"Hey, Jade," he called out as I strode into the server station, tightening his apron strings.

I nodded. "Jasper." The staff weren't stupid, they knew our relationship had become more outside the boundaries of the restaurant, but we still tried to keep it reigned in.

"Last night."

A pen flew in my direction and I tossed him a notepad. "Last night." I knew it was sad to say it, but a part of me was going to miss coming here. It wasn't a huge part, but still. It was my adult conversation job.

But I tried not to think about that, serving my customers, some of which had become regulars in my section. It was neat to act the part of a happy-go-lucky, still green, serving machine, aka Jade. But the apron would be tied for the last time. And tonight was the last night I'd wear that green polo shirt, and I can't say I was bothered at all by that. In fact, by the time I finished my shift, I was glad to be free of it.

I fell into the booth, and Jasper slid in beside me. Evanora sat across from me. No one spoke until Niall walked over.

He dropped the envelope in front of Evanora before presenting us with ours. "Your record of employments will be mailed out to you, along with your final cheques. You should have everything within a week or so, and if not, give me a call."

"Won't you join us?" Jasper asked, pointing at the spot beside Evanora.

"Nah. I don't do goodbyes." He went to say something more but stopped. "Have a good night." Niall turned and walked to the back.

"I don't do goodbyes either," Evanora said. "It's been fun working with you both." She started to slip out of the booth.

"Evanora?" I asked, reaching for her arm. "Since I'm leaving now, would it be possible to find out your real name?"

She stared at my arm like I'd tasered her.

In shock and defence, I pulled it back.

"Did we become friends somewhere along the way and I missed it?"

I blinked, and my jaw dropped. "Um, no."

"There's your answer." With a spring in her step, she headed for the doors. "Oh, enjoy Lethbridge. You'll be missed."

"And that," Jasper said, pointing in her direction, "was probably the nicest thing to ever come out of her mouth. Hell may have just frozen over."

"Wow." I wrapped my hand around the envelope. "I can't say I'm going to miss her."

"Told you." Korey stood and extended his hand. "Come on. Let's go home."

We walked up hand in hand to my apartment, after checking that the U-Haul van loosely packed with Korey's stuff was still secure. A duffle bag was all he brought into my place. It was enough to get him through the next two nights and the drive south. I envied how lightly he packed.

"I seriously need a shower. To completely wipe the Westside smell off me." I rummaged through my suitcase packed with enough clothes to get me to my new destination and grabbed my nighttime clothes.

Korey stood at the bathroom door. "May I join you?"

I let my gaze linger on his handsome face. So sweet and yet rugged. A man's man if ever there was one. Allowing my eyes to drift south for a heartbeat, I nodded. Setting my glasses on the counter, I allowed him to slowly pull my nasty green polo free of my waist, slipping it up and over my head and letting it fall onto the floor. It would be safe to say it wouldn't get packed into my suitcase.

Once free of my black pants, I straightened up, shoulders back, breasts high and perky. His eyes devoured me in one fell swoop.

He unbuckled his pants and they slid quickly to the floor. Kicking them off to the side, he tugged his shirt off and stood there.

My hands couldn't wait to touch his body. So perfect and strong, and yet tender when needed.

He twirled me around, and unclasped my bra, pushing the straps over my shoulders with his lips. The electricity surged through my veins and pooled in my feminine places. Hooking a finger through my g-string, he slid his hands over my hips, kissing my back the lower he went.

I threw my head back. "I'm so dirty." It came out as a purr.

As he straightened up, his hands trailed up my thighs, stopping at the top. His fingers danced to the middle, and I wrapped an arm around his head. "Oh, yes you are," he whispered in my ears. "You're a very dirty lady."

Instinctually I moaned as his fingers found the sweet spot, the sexiness of it all pooling between my thighs. He pressed in closer to me, and I felt his excitement. Neither of us could wait.

As his fingers moved and played, I bent over the

bathroom counter, his arms still wrapped around me.

Every movement of his body against mine filled my soul. Every breath he exhaled, I breathed it in, savouring everything I could. His sweat soaked body was the most erotic scent I'd ever smelled, so musky and spicy. Hands so huge they could seriously hurt someone, were gentle and tantalizing, never missing a square inch of my heated skin. Korey was the master of cleaning, and after our sexy shower there wasn't a dirty spot left on my body. Or his.

But it was impossible to dry me off.

Free to be uncovered and laying naked beside him, I snuggled into him, putting my wet head upon his shoulder. A light breeze from the window blew across my body, cooling the tiny droplets of water still on my singed skin. The full moon peeked in on us, the white glow paling his sun-drenched tan.

"So tomorrow…" Korey began, his arm tightening around me. "Your family's coming to help bring your stuff into the van, correct?"

"Yeah. Around one." I swallowed. Nervous little butterflies took up flight in my stomach. "About that."

"It's okay. I'll let Dina do it her way and I'll try not to ruffle her feathers too much." He tangled his fingers through my damp hair.

Dina and I had mended together our fight. It was a mutual acceptance on both our parts that I was exhausted and overwhelmed. That, and no matter what I did, Dina could never stay mad at me. I was the grudge carrier, whereas she let it all slide off her back. It was a good system, because it didn't take much for her to forgive me, and then that's when I caved. She knew me too well.

"It's not Dina. It's me." My heart pounded relentlessly against my rib cage.

"Oh yeah?" His arm tugged out from under me and he rolled over to face me. "What's on your mind?"

"The move." I stared at his chest. It was too painful to

search out his eyes and if I saw any hurt in them, I'd probably start crying.

His chest filled and deflated, and a sigh came out with it. "I was afraid of this." He rolled onto his back. "I knew it was coming, I just hoped it came after."

"After?"

"Yeah, after we'd settled into our apartment. Once you saw how perfect it would all be, maybe you'd see it wasn't so bad."

My bottom lip quivered, and I bit it to stop it. I didn't know what to say though.

If Korey knew I was nervous, he hadn't said anything. In fact, it was the reverse. He'd gone on and on about how a fresh start was a good thing, how it had encouraged him to break out of his comfort zone and live life. Over breakfasts, he'd pour over Google images of the new neighbourhood and point out nearby sights. He wondered what the neighbours would be like. But it had all been him. I hadn't shared that enthusiasm.

My chin tucked into my chest. "I've tried. Really I have."

"Maybe." He stared up at the ceiling. "Maybe not." I snuggled into him, but he wiggled out from under me. "Don't."

"Don't what?"

"Don't try to soften the blow by being kind. Just tell me what's on your mind." His voice was gruff and a touch harsh.

But I'd caused it. This was all on me, and I had to step up and own it. Even if it hurt. "I can't do it."

He huffed and sat on the edge of the bed, his back to me. The moonlight highlighted the tautness of hard muscles. "At all?" His voice drifted away.

I shook my head and the tears fell. "I'm sorry."

His head fell into his hands and his back curled. I wanted to reach out and touch him, but figured I'd be shunned. "For how long?"

"I don't know if I'll ever be ready."

The dreads flopped back and forth. "Not that. How long have you felt like this?" He turned to face me but kept his distance.

"A while. I've tried, really, I have. When I talk to people, I try to sound excited, but it hurts too much when I think about leaving."

"But you've given notice at your jobs, and this place."

"I know." My voice tried to gain strength, but the cracks in it gave away my heartache. "Because I was trying to do the right thing. I was trying to make you happy. I was trying to be everything you needed."

"Oh Shayne, you're already everything I need. That's why I'm doing this. Moving to a new place to start a new life. With you."

"But I can't go."

"Is it me?"

"Not at all." I reached out to him, but he inched himself back. "I love you."

"So, it's all about the move."

"Totally."

He slumped further, deflated and hurt. His eyes shone in the glow of the night. "And if I were to stay here, there'd be no issue."

I'd thought about that and circulated those ideas through my head. Korey and I could move into a new place, one that was new to us both. We could start new jobs, maybe even career-orientated ones. But it had to be here. My family was here. Everything I needed, everything I was used to, was here. And I knew I'd be happy. But I didn't think Korey would be. He liked drifting, not being committed to anything for too long.

I clutched my hands together. "I've contemplated that, and where I think I'd be happy with that situation, you wouldn't be." I swallowed. "A huge part of me worries you'll get tired of me and leave me, so when that happens, at least I'll have my support system right here."

Another loud huff escaped from him. "What's with you assuming I'll leave you?" He rose from the bed. "You've already left me."

"No, I haven't." My voice pleaded, but my brain registered what he said. By me not wanting to move, in his eyes, I had already left.

Korey grabbed his duffle bag off the floor and stormed away.

Scrambling to find something to pull on, I felt the softness of a t-shirt and whipped it on. It barely covered my ass, but at least it was covered. "Korey," I yelled.

He'd stopped at the open door, buttoning a pair of jeans close. "What?"

"Please don't go."

"Why? You have. Only you haven't truly left, and you will never leave. You're a coward. Afraid to try something new. And I can't be with a coward who's already left." He stepped beyond the boundaries of the door, into the hallway. "As soon as I can, I'll send back your deposit."

"Korey, please," I cried. Tears streamed down my cheeks. "Please. I love you."

"But love isn't enough, Shayne."

My heart shattered with each step he took. The further the distance, the more damage. I closed the door and carried myself back to the bedroom. Outside the window in the vacant stillness of the night, I heard the rumblings of the diesel-fueled moving van fire up, and the screech of the tires as it sped out of the parking lot.

Chapter Twenty-One

The morning came with a giant FU. My neck snapped with a wicked kink and sent a stabbing pain right up into my brain. A dull headache formed, and I was suddenly mad with the world. Climbing out of bed, I went to the bathroom but froze as I passed the mirror. My eyes were puffy and the dark circles under were packed with enough luggage for a week's holiday. With the condition of the rat's nest atop my head, there wasn't enough detangler to undo that mess.

Empty and drained, I surveyed my apartment. Aside from the bedroom in which I only had to pack up the sheets and pillows into the open box, everything was ready for a move. Boxes with their rigid numbering system and order stared at me, taunting me, telling me what a dumbass I was.

I kicked a box over and got dressed while attempting to make myself presentable. Walking over to the rental office, I inhaled, hoping for a yes.

I stepped into the squat little room, no bigger than my bedroom. A long peninsula separated me from the two desks and one grouchy-looking lady, who frantically typed on the keyboard while chatting with someone over her headset about the lack of available space. My heart plummeted into my intestines. A desktop fan blew stale air in my direction.

She snapped her head up to me. "Rental cheques go in that mailbox." Her short stubby finger pointed to a bright yellow mailbox hanging on the far wall.

"It's not that. I gave my notice last month and my last day's today, but I was wondering if there are any available apartments? I'd like to stay."

"Everything's rented out. What apartment?" She typed feverishly.

"12D."

The keys beneath her fingers clicked. "Yeah. Yours is already waiting for someone else and your move out is at three."

"I know."

The bells on the door sounded behind me, and a couple walked in.

"Can I help you?" the lady said to them.

My legs weakened, and I braced myself against the counter. This was not the place to fall apart. I excused myself, inching past the young couple and back out into the fresh air, heartache spreading through me like a bad disease. As I headed back up to my apartment, I sent out a general text to my family. *Move cancelled. Stay home. I'll explain later.*

I hadn't even put my key in the lock when my phone rang. "Hey, Sean." My voice betrayed my greeting.

"What's going on?"

"I couldn't do it. I can't leave." I closed the door and banged my head against it. It didn't help my headache, but oddly enough it felt good.

"Where are you?"

"My place."

"And Korey?"

"He left last night. Probably in Lethbridge already."

"Stay there. I'm on my way."

"I don't have any place to go," I whispered, fresh tears staining my cheeks.

I hadn't moved from the doorway when he buzzed; my phone still clenched in my hand and my head against the door. When he knocked on it a minute later, I'm not sure why I jumped.

Pulling it open, I stepped back.

"Oh, my little Shaney Bear," he said as he walked in, arms ready to wrap around me. He had always called me that as a child, usually when I was sad and he was trying to get me to smile. It never worked then and didn't work now.

I cuddled into my big brother. "I'm an idiot."

"You're not an idiot, trust me. I've never thought that."

"But he's gone."

"Explain to me what happened."

And I did. I left out the sexcapades in the bathroom and shower but replayed almost word for word the rest.

He wiped his brow. "Well, first things first. Let's get you out of here."

"And where am I going to go?"

"You'll move into the basement."

"Of your house?"

"You know of another?" He pursed his lips together.

I didn't. "That's like a step back in my life."

"Well you have two options. Run after Korey…"

I shook my head knowing full well I couldn't live there.

"Or move in, temporarily…" He stressed the last word, "Until you find a new place. There are lots of apartments out there. We can shop tomorrow. But first things first." He pulled out his phone and texted into the group message. It pinged onto my phone. *Move back on. Change of locations. Meet at Shayne's for 1. Empty your vehicles – we need the space.*

"Now, we're going to load up my truck and take a trip to my house."

"Thank you," I said as my thoughts drifted to Korey. I wondered if he was at the apartment, or if he'd stopped somewhere along the way. The sigh that breezed out from me aided in further cracking my heart.

A few hours later, my boxes and furniture lined the wall of Sean and Randy's unfinished basement -- Dina, Xander and my parents long gone. The basics—my suitcase and a box of clothes—sat in their spare bedroom on the main floor.

"Now here's the rules."

I raised my eyebrow at Randy. "I'm three weeks away from turning twenty. Aren't I a little old for rules?" Besides I wasn't even technically living there, just temporary like a hotel stay or something.

"You're not too old for these ones."

I stood in the threshold of the spare room, hands crossed across my chest. "Okay." I braced myself for curfews and housecleaning duties, although helping out was a given.

"You're to join us for breakfast every morning at eight, whether you like it or not," he said to the disgusted look I planted on my face. "You're to change clothes every twelve hours. No moping around unwashed and frumpy for days on end. I get it, you're upset, and we'll allow you to grieve that relationship loss, however, changing your clothes is good for your mental health."

I supposed that much was true. Nodding, it was a sign to continue with the rules.

"We'll be apartment shopping soon. As it's the end of the month, we'll give the buildings a chance to clear out and clean up. The job search will begin in three days. Fair enough?"

He was being more than fair, and I was grateful. I was still expected some sort of a curfew. "That's it?"

"Do you need more?" He raised a brow at me.

I shook my head. Three days to mope, with clothes changing, and then it was time to move on.

"Good, then enjoy your stay." A smile crossed his face and he hugged me. "It'll be nice having you around. Help yourself to anything you need, but if you finish something off, write it on the list hanging on the fridge."

"I can handle that." Easy enough. I surveyed the running list. My first trip out, I'd start with picking up the items they had scribbled down.

Randy walked into the kitchen and turned abruptly. "Oh,

if you want a nice bath, use ours. Just give us a heads' up first. We have nice smelling salts and soaks up there. The bath off your room is a joke." Yeah, the standard sized tubs weren't ideal for relaxing in. "I'll get you a spare key too, so you can come and go as you please."

"Thanks, Randy." I leaned on the counter as he prepped a bottle.

The bottle warmer clicked on. "My door's always open if you want to talk."

"I know. Thank you."

"And for what it's worth, you both made a mistake. He shouldn't have left, but you should've gone." He stared me hard in the eyes. "Your family loves you, and we know you love us back. We'll always be here. This isn't ten years ago when Sean left. There's Skype and Facetime. There will always be contact. Don't be afraid to spread your wings and fly." He tapped me on the nose and walked up to his bedroom.

Spreading my wings and flying away? Easier said than done. But I supposed he was partly in the right.

Chapter Twenty-Two

"Ugh." I slammed the lid on my laptop. For the last couple of hours, under the pretense of job hunting, I'd been searching all of Lily's social media pages, seeing if she'd commented on a friend's status, if she checked in someplace. Anything. It had been radio silence now for six weeks. I hung my head.

"What's that?" Sean asked walking into the kitchen.

"I was checking for signs of life from Lily."

"And?" He poured himself another cup of coffee.

"Nothing."

"I'm sure she's okay."

I rested my elbows on the table. "How can you know?"

He pulled out a chair, quietly so as not awaken Scarlett. "I can just hope that whatever was going through her head, she's okay. This will sound terrible, but I'm glad she walked away from her problems rather than harming the children or herself."

That was true. There was a recent story in the news about a mom who couldn't take it anymore and rather than pull a Lily, drowned each of her kids before she took her own life.

"Still."

A big brotherly pat to my arm. "It's still not easy and I get that."

"Thank you." That was all I wanted. Acknowledgement that it wasn't easy. I lost my best friend and my boyfriend within a month. I'd been forced to temporarily move in with my brother. My little adventure I'd seen in my future had gone up in a puff of smoke. For now. I just needed to wait out a few more weeks until the start of college, and then hopefully my adventure would start.

"Find any kind of job?" It sounded like a jab, but I knew it wasn't. Although we'd fallen into a rhythm over the last two weeks, I was still an intrusion to their regular lives. At least before Scarlett. Chaos seemed to be the new norm.

"I'll never find anything." I didn't know much about the recession aside from job scarcity, and I kicked myself for not paying attention when Korey went on and on about it. Was I ever going to find a normal job? "I did communicate with a couple of pregnant ladies on a birthing forum. After I take my doula course this weekend, they said they would be interested in meeting with me."

"Not to be a Debbie Downer, but is that consistent work? Could you pay your rent off that?" That big brotherly tone shined through loud and clear.

"Not at first. Maybe after I've attended a few births?"

"And until that point?"

I sighed and stood, stretching my arms above my head. There had been some mental debate about going back to Westside, as I knew I'd left them understaffed, but I couldn't do it. That's where I met Korey. He belonged there before I did. And he wasn't there. He was in Lethbridge, ignoring my texts and calls. I hoped the job was treating him well. "I'll keep looking and dropping off resumes. Something's bound to show up." It may be a job at McDonald's, but at least it would be something.

"What time's the apartment viewing?"

"Two."

"Mind if I come with you?"

"Never."

A couple of hours later, Sean joined me as we toured the tiny 600 sq. foot one-bedroom apartment. It had a functional kitchen and a bedroom barely big enough to hold my queen-sized mattress. The paint was newer, but the carpet was a relic from decades gone by. Amenities were zero, and the walls were paper-thin as I learned the next-door neighbour's name is Janine. Still, it was within my feeble price range.

"I'll take it."

The building manager lit up, probably because it had been empty for months and the neighbourhood was rundown. What options did I have?

"Great. You can move in tomorrow?" It was more a question than any sort of an option. If anything, I'd prefer to wait until the end of the month.

"Give us a minute?" Sean pulled me off to the side, over to the big window in the living room. There wasn't even a patio door. "What's going on?"

I shook my head and forced some cheer into my words. "Nothing. I'm going to sign a tenant agreement." The space around me could be quite cozy, if I put some love into it.

Love. That's what Korey and I had planned for our place. Lots of love to make the space us. A little chic, a little homey, but pieces of both of us. Tears welled up in my eyes, and I turned away.

Sean walked over to the building manager. "Can she think about it? Take twenty-four hours to mull it over?"

She scoffed a little and raised her voice to be higher than a whisper. "Well, I do have other potential tenants checking it out tomorrow."

"If it's meant to be, she'll be in contact before that." Sean made his way back to me, and I wiped my eyes. "Let's go home and talk about this amazing place."

Always one to be kind, even though the place was a dump at best, Sean pointed out the positives on the way out the door like how the crack in the wall could be a line of mountains in the distance if it was painted. However, upon descending the stairs he pointed out how the place came with its own fragrance, urine-soaked carpet.

Yeah, I wasn't going to sign any lease or agreement. This would never be my home.

I climbed behind the steering wheel and shoved my keys into the ignition.

Sean slipped in beside me. "What's on your mind?"

I let the tears burst from their holds. "I miss him so much. I know we were only together for a short time, months barely, but…" He was my everything. And he was gone.

"So, call him."

I smeared mascara across my face. "I have. And texted him. And I even mailed him a letter."

"I don't know what to say." Sean hung his head. He'd had maybe two or three semi-serious relationships before Randy. And he just knew Randy was the one. He knew it from the second date.

Is that what I was feeling? Was Korey my one? I sniffed and dried my eyes on the shoulder of my shirt, mascara wiping off. Oh well, I needed to do laundry anyways. "I just want to go home and think."

"I understand." The knowing nod and quick squeeze on my arm told me he did.

Problem was, as wonderful as his home was, it wasn't *my* home, and I didn't belong there.

###

A few days later, I rolled out of bed. The house was eerily quiet, but it was two am. I had yet to sleep. There was so much on my mind.

Now that I had taken a doula course, I was excited and actively trying to recruit clients, and trying to come up with a business name. My instructor had outlined a game plan for the truly dedicated. If this was something to make a career out of, within a year of hard work and dedication, I could make a decent living. It was a goal. In the meantime, I still needed a regular job. And as much as I wasn't eager about it, a job interview with an indoor amusement park had me booked for a 9:45 am interview in three days.

But that wasn't what was truly keeping me awake.

Today was my birthday. I was twenty now. Officially out of my teens. My childhood behind me as my adulthood stretched out ahead of me. I wished as I was excited for it. I wished I could celebrate it with Korey. I wished we were together.

Headphones plugged in, I tiptoed as quietly as I could through the kitchen and living room to the back deck. I put my hand on the knob and twisted, and with a quick shoulder to the door, pushed it open with only the slightest bit of a creaking. Damn door was more a giveaway to intruders than any bell. I'd only hoped Sean and Randy were soundly sleeping and didn't hear.

The sky was cloudy, and a pale orange glow from the reflected city lights surrounded me. It was peaceful, as I saw clearly in the backyard and nothing sinister hid in the shadows. I sat on the couch and stretched out, breathing in the summer air. Earphones in, I thumbed through my music and hit the playlist marked 'Korey'; a collection of country and belly-dancing songs. Immersed in the beats of a familiar country that I now knew all the words to, my foot tapped out the rhythm and I allowed myself to fall under the spell of a powerful memory.

Of dancing in the dining room. Of laughter. Of seeing the way his face lit up as I fumbled on a two-step.

I flipped through my photo roll, stopping and staring into the perfect browns of a man who'd stolen my heart. The two of us, his arms wrapped around me, poised and ready to kiss my cheek. The funny faces we made. He made the perfect duck face and I laughed until the tears rolled.

Every night was the same. The music, the photos, the memories. I figured it would help. If I did it so many times, eventually I'd get sick of him. Instead, it made the longing worse. The hole in my heart deepened.

He never called or returned my texts. I wanted to know what he was doing. Was he happy? Was the job what he envisioned? Did he miss me the way I missed him? Did he crave me like I craved him? Was his heart as shattered as mine?

A lightbulb went off over my head, and I opened my browser. I knew what I had to do. And I had to at least try. If it was a bust, then I could let it go, and try to move on. But, if there was even a morsel of hope, then I'd be staying to work it out.

With a few clicks, my flight was booked to Lethbridge. And it left in two hours.

Chapter Twenty-Three

Six hours after booking my ticket, I stepped off the plane and followed the trickle of passengers into the terminal. With a hop in my step, I scooted through the baggage pickup and out the door, hailing the first cab I saw.

Climbing in the taxi and plugging my nose from the overpowering pine stench, I gave him the address of the apartment Korey and I'd signed a lease on a little over a month ago. However, the sadness and fear were gone. I missed him more than I possibly imagined I could. I knew my heart belonged with him, no matter where the location was.

"Can you go a little faster please?" I bounced my feet on the floorboards in the back seat.

As the cabbie drove through town, I was impressed by how much this place resembled my hometown and wasn't as alien as I'd thought. We passed by strip malls, with familiar named stores and residential areas lined with huge trees. It was amazing how similar it was, even though the city itself was much smaller than my hometown. I'm not sure what I expected, but this wasn't it. As we drove across the river, I started to grasp the idea that this could be my home. It seemed to have everything I was used to back home.

There was no family here and no Korey back home. But love won out and after weeks apart, it was clear I needed Korey. I missed him more each day. Like Randy said, my family would always be around whenever I needed, but I couldn't let Korey get away.

I tapped the cabbie on the shoulder. "Are we almost there?" My destiny awaited.

"Nearly. Two minutes." He tapped on the dash.

He drove through an idyllic area, nestled away from the university but well within view, and parked outside the building. It looked different than the images I'd seen, but I chalked it up to being because I was there in person. Pictures are close, but never a replacement for the real thing. I should know. Korey's pictures weren't the same. Even as I lay in bed with his face staring at me from my phone, it wasn't the same as the living and breathing being I desperately wanted to snuggle against.

I paid the cabbie and grabbed my bag. Checking the time – it was after eight—I turned around and stopped him before he drove away. "Just hang tight for a minute, just in case."

"Sure thing, Lady." He put the taxi into park.

Nervousness, but of the good kind, powered me to the door. I pressed the buzzer for apartment 302. No response. Was he already at work? I pressed the buzzer again hoping he was just sleeping and needed to be woken up.

Nothing.

Shoulders weighted down with worry, I walked over to the cab and slipped into the back seat. "I need to go to the bank please."

He opened the GPS on the dash. "Which one?"

"Treasures."

He typed it in. "Which location?"

Stunned, I tried to remember. I didn't think Lethbridge was big enough for two branches within that bank. "I don't know. Which is closest?" He'd never mentioned the possibilities of two, but then again, I'd never thought to ask. In my little mind, I'd picture Lethbridge as this tiny little place and it was turning out to be so much more.

"Stafford."

Guess we'll go by distance first. "Let's try that one." I picked the one that appeared as if it were closer, and therefore easier, to get to.

My phone pinged with an incoming message.

Rule One. Breakfast is at 8. You'd better have a good excuse for not being here.

My smile was as large as the river valley we were crossing over. My fingers typed quickly. *There is. I'm in Lethbridge.*

Sean typed back. *I'm very pleased to hear it.*

My heart fluttered in my chest. I was going home, and I couldn't get there fast enough. Thankfully, the bank was a short jaunt away.

"Shall I wait?" The cabbie asked, pulling up in front of the quaintly-sized branch. The full kitchen at Westside was larger.

"If I'm not back in five minutes, feel free to leave." I paid in full plus extra for the wait, the empty minutes slowly draining my 'spare' cash.

"Good luck, lady," he called out as I walked away.

I opened the heavy door into the vestibule and peered through the metal gates, frantically searching for anyone working. Banging against grey barrier, I caught the attention of a worker. "Excuse me, I'm looking for Korey Duhamel."

"Who?"

"Korey. Duhamel." I slowed down my speech to catch my breath. Maybe it came out jumbled the first time. "He's new."

She was older, like my parents' age, but dressed as someone befitting a bank, in a blazer, white blouse and dress pants. "I'm sorry, I can't help you." She turned away from me.

"Please." I pleaded, hoping the plea in my voice would cause her to look at me and see how desperate I was. "I just flew in to see him. He's my boyfriend."

Eyes narrowed in my direction, and then glanced up toward the ceiling. I assume our conversation was being heavily monitored.

"Maybe I have the wrong bank." My heart fell, and I

pulled out my phone. "He looks like this." I opened the picture of us, one of my favourites, and pushed it against an opening in the gates I'd hoped was large enough to see without interference. "That's my Korey."

Recognition settled on her face and she stepped closer. "Oh, him. He's new."

I nodded. What I really wanted to do was bang my head against the gate, but I held back. "You know him?"

"Yeah. Funny guy. Asks us to call him Kaumaha."

"That's him," I said, a smile cracking across my face. "Is he here?"

"No."

Dammit. I was never going to get any answers quickly.

"He took a couple days off for family emergency. He went home."

My shoulders rolled inwards, and my heart deflated like a popped balloon. My savings had taken a hit with the last-minute airline ticket, there was no way I couldn't afford to fly to William's Lake, and even if I did, I wouldn't have the foggiest idea where to find him. "Thanks," I told her, and staggered out of the building.

There was a bench outside the door, and I felt I needed to sit and regroup. This wasn't how it worked in the movies. If the girl chased the guy, he was at the end, ready to be surprised. Instead, it's me who's surprised because the guy wasn't even here. Oh, what was I going to do?

Family emergency? What could've gone on? Did something happen to Harry, or to Marcus? I had no idea. I couldn't imagine Williams Lake having more than one hospital, but I'd been wrong about Lethbridge. Maybe I should call and ask. I opened my browser and searched for the hospital, closing it just as quickly. As if they'd tell me anything. Sheesh. What a pickle.

Instead, I dialled the number for the local cab, and while waiting for it to arrive, I texted Sean.

Jokes on me. He's not even here. Family emergency back home.

It took a minute, but he finally responded. *So now what?*

I sighed. *IDK*. Frick. What was I going to do? *I'm coming home.* With my heavy heart in a wet handbag of tears. Dammit, maybe I should've said something ahead of time. Sent a text or something. What a waste of time and precious resources.

When a new cab pulled up, I slinked into the backseat. "The airport, please." Although my lips stayed sealed, anger within me threatened to surge. I was mad at myself. If I'd not been such a coward before, I wouldn't be in this predicament.

One foot in front of the other, my pride trailing behind me, I purchased a ticket back home. Another expensive ticket, even though I was going as standby. My little whim was costing me all the money I had saved for college, and it would take more than a few shifts at the amusement park to restock my bank account. It would take a month, at least. Foolishly I'd hoped I'd get to cancel that interview.

I grabbed a shitty, overpriced breakfast at one of the kiosks in the terminal and gulped it down. It may have cost more than I'll make in an hour, but it was surprisingly tasty. With a smoothie in my hand, I walked up to the check-in counter.

"Checking for standby room." I had my ID ready, in case I got lucky.

The airline personnel typed in the computer.

Surveying the area, the passengers that had been seated at the gate before I got breakfast, and there weren't many, had already boarded. I kept my fingers crossed. I just wanted to get home and melt into a puddled mess.

"We can get you on. Lots of room. You'll have a stop over in Calgary."

"Whatever." The longest trip was always the return trip home. It never failed.

She typed again after checking my ID and a ticket dispensed from the printer. "Seat 13B. Enjoy your flight. Oh, and happy birthday."

"Thanks." I plugged headphones into my phone and selected an album, ignoring my usual playlist. Besides, listening to it would cause the tears to fall fast and furious and I didn't need to have my impending breakdown in public. It wasn't going to be a long flight to Calgary, but I wanted to zone out just the same. Something to take my mind off the situation as much as I could.

The birthing podcasts ought to work. I needed to listen and focus on the mechanics of birth, which as I learned over the weekend, was highly fascinating.

As I walked out onto the tarmac and over to the plane, the sun beat down on me, rendering me nearly blind, and the monotone voice playing in my ears drowned out the voices of the airport personnel keeping me between the lines. All I wanted was to get into the tiny little jet that sat in all its glory. Tromping up the stairs and into the darkened interior of the plane, I flashed my boarding pass at the thirty-something male flight attendant, who stood in front of the captain and pilot.

"Good morning." He checked my ticket. "To the back, right side," he said with a point.

I inhaled a sharp pang of regret, and the stale airplane air didn't help. Even with the front door open, the recycled air hadn't fully dissipated. Inching my way down the narrow aisle, I passed a few men in business suits and a couple of ladies. The plane was largely empty. No kidding there was room.

Row 13. As empty and blue as my soul. The entire row was devoid of people and I, for one, was happy. No one to make idle chit-chat with and no one I needed to put up with. I tossed my untouched overnight bag into the overhead storage and flumped down into the window seat.

While I thumbed out a text, the flight attendant stopped at my row and tapped on his ear.

I removed the earbud.

"I'm sorry, miss, but you'll need to turn off your device." His hand rested on the seat in front of me, but a sincere expression filled his face. He was only doing his job, and I couldn't fault him for that.

"Will do." As soon as he walked away, I finished a group

text to Sean and Randy. *On the plane. Landing at YYC in 45. Will confirm when I get there the next steps home. Coming on standby.*

Randy was the first to respond. *Sorry it didn't work out.*

Not as sorry as I was. The tears built up, and the ache in my heart spread. It wasn't a numb feeling like I wanted, I was very much aware how much everything hurt. Breathing was hard. My chest hurt, and my extremities had an unfamiliar tingle. I pulled my legs up into a hug and rested my chin on top.

The flight attendant walked by again and gave me a look, this one came with more of a warning.

"It's not even on." I even flashed my phone to prove it and gave my eyes a wipe. "I'm just keeping the earphones in so I won't be bothered."

He stopped and walked back to the end of my row. "You okay?"

I shook my head and glanced out the window onto the tarmac. "It's been a long day."

"It's only nine-thirty in the morning," he said.

"Precisely." I closed my eyes, feeling the hot rivers streaming down. A moment later, there was a gentle tap on my shoulder. Opening my eyes, I looked up.

The flight attendant passed me a personal pack of tissues.

"Thanks." The tears kept falling. The need to explain my soul-crushing sadness was overwhelming. I didn't fall apart like this, at least not in public. My misery was usually left to the sanctity of my bedroom. "Ever been in love?" Clearly, headphones or not, I was desperate to talk to someone, and this gentleman working the early flight was my target.

He nodded. "Absolutely. Got me a fine lady at home."

"That's great." I forced a smile and swallowed down a massive lump that had wedged itself in my throat. "I flew here from Edmonton to surprise my man and tell him how much I love him and how I'm ready to move here to be with him, and it turns out he's not even here." My breath caught in my throat. "I don't even know where he went."

His gaze stayed focused on me until something caught his attention, and he nodded to someone at the front of the plane. "I'm truly sorry. I need to prepare for takeoff." He wore a sympathetic smile, but for a moment, I was glad for the company. "I'll come back. Promise." The flight attendant gave my shoulder a quick pat.

I looked back out the window and watched as the ground crew fluttered around, moving cables and connectors. Everything they did had purpose; the way everything came together with a goal. Nothing I did lately made much sense. What a mess I was.

"Excuse me, you came all this way for love?"

That voice.

I whipped my head around and came face to face with him. "Korey," I said, my lips erupting into a canyon-wide smile as I tried focusing through the blur. Even through that, it was easy to see his dreads were gone, and he sported a rugged model look. I blinked several times and wiped my eyes on one of the tissues the nice flight attendant had brought.

Able to see clearly, I can't say the lack of dreads suited Korey, but it did make his eyes pop even more, even though they were ringed with a darkness I related to. "What are you doing here? Where'd you come from?" I'd done a quick scan while I walked to my seat and didn't see him. Mind you, I hadn't been looking either.

"I should be asking you that."

"Come sit." I wiped my eyes again and patted the seat beside me. Hardly a heartbeat passed, and he was beside me. It had been a long time since I'd breathed the same air as him. "I came to say I'm sorry. I should've come down with you. I should've trusted in you more to know I'd be okay. I was so lonely without you, it hurt." I covered my chest with my hand. "I'm sorry I was a coward." My mouth sputtered out words a mile a minute and my blood pulsed just as fast. I reached for his hand, so soft and warm and like a repressed idiot, I grabbed it and touched it to my cheek. God, he smelled good.

He turned his fingers against my skin and trailed them

down slowly. "I've missed you. So much."

"I've missed you too." I placed a kiss into his palm. "When you get back, can we talk and try again?" I wanted to start from scratch or at least from a point from before he walked out of my apartment.

"When I get back?" He held my face in his gaze, curiosity rolling off it.

"Yeah a lady at the bank said you took a couple days off for a family emergency."

"That I did." He twisted in his seat as the plane jolted with the push back.

The flight attendant walked past and stopped, a grin forming.

I beamed and squeezed Korey's hand, looking up at the flight attendant. "This is him, my man."

"I'm so pleased. Fasten your seatbelt, sir." He walked out of sight.

Korey complied, and I gave mine a tighten.

I leaned my head against his. "So, your emergency? Is it Marcus or Harry?"

Deep wrinkles settled in the corners of his eyes as he smiled. "Neither of them, thankfully. You're my emergency."

My jaw dropped. I was hardly anyone's emergency.

"Shayne, it's your birthday, and I couldn't be without you one more day. I was flying home to see you and see if we can start over." He searched my eyes. "If you still want me."

"Oh, I want you." It was hard to see him as tears of joy clouded my view of the most amazing man I knew. "But what about the job?"

"I hate it." He pointed to his head. "Had to cut the dreads."

"What, they can't make you do that?" They couldn't, right? That was a huge issue, similar to not hiring someone based on race. When he ran his fingers through what was left of his dark hair, I wanted to do the same to see if it was still soft but held myself back.

"They can't but I was strongly coerced into it. The branch manager's an asshole and keeps dropping the word nepotism into every conversation. He accuses me of not being a team player because I refuse to fit in and blend. Oh, yeah, and how I probably run to daddy every time there's an issue."

Yeah, I couldn't picture that. Korey was a team player, and I'd witnessed that on many occasions. He made Westside fun.

"But I conformed. I cut the dreads off to prove a point and even started wearing suits."

I reached out and ran my fingers through his hair.

"It's just hair. And I can grow it back." With the dreads gone, he looked so different. More mature, for sure. "You look different too."

"How so?" Probably worse. Much worse. I hadn't cried so much in all my life.

"Like you're figuring things out."

A weak laugh breathed out of me with that comment. "I completed a doula course, and I'm seeking out clients."

His face lit up. "That's great. What about college plans?"

"I postponed. Again." That had been a fun conversation, but what were my parents going to do? Ground me? "The adventure I thought I needed or thought I'd get wasn't on the college grounds. That wasn't going to be mine to enjoy. My adventure lay elsewhere, I just didn't realise it."

He cleared his throat. "Oh, yeah? Tell me more."

"You're my adventure." I squeezed his hand in mine. "And I want it to start as soon as possible."

"Like now?"

"Yep. Right here in row thirteen."

He leaned forward, the distance between us measured in mere inches. "And living accommodations?"

"You could move to the moon, and I'd follow you. I love you, Korey."

"And I love you." His hand cupped my cheek, his lips

within kissing distance. "You were right. I can get a job anywhere. Those real jobs aren't me. I'm not happy there. I was happy with you, and I want that for us. Let's make it work. Here, there or anywhere, because I need you."

I'd never kissed anyone on a plane before, and certainly never during take off. You could say our relationship got wings and took flight. And you'd be right.

Serving Up DEVOTION

Chapter One

I don't understand why people think I'm a bitch. Yes, I'm abrupt and to the point, and have no problem telling you what I think, when or if I'm asked, and sometimes, even when I'm not. I don't put in long hours on my feet in a dead-end job to make friends or find love. I wished to hell people would just let me do the job I've been doing for years without the expectation of more; more laughter in the server station; more sweetness in my words; more of everything I don't care to give and am not required to. So that makes me a bitch? If that's how people want to see it, then fine, I can live with it. It's not like those people are my friends anyway. Just let me put in my hours and go home. That's where my heart is anyway.

"When are you getting new help, Niall?" I slammed my empty tray on the table beside the computer a little louder than I'd intended. Customers didn't notice, but it sure made my manager startle. He looked me over as I waited expectantly for answers I knew I wouldn't get. At least not ones I wanted to hear.

Niall looked like crap. He slumped more than usual, and his eyes wore tired like a neon sign. He wasn't used to waiting tables, but for the last few weeks we'd been short staffed, and he came out onto the floor to help us out. Well, good for him. If he'd hired staff by now, I wouldn't be so irritable and overworked, and he could go back to doing whatever it was I kept pulling him away from.

I tapped my foot, and Niall looked back to the screen. "Damn, that supper rush was crazy. I forgot how demanding being on the front end was, especially trying to keep the floor running smoothly. I'll punch in L7's order, and you can finish it up for me." When I didn't move he looked over and sighed, "I'm sorry, but the applications just aren't rolling in."

"Any help is better than no help, right? I can't keep going on like this." I stuck the notepad into my apron and marched around the wall that separated the front end from the tiny server station, calling over my shoulder, "As of next week, I'm back to working a max of six shifts a week. Double shifts on the weekend are a no-go."

"Evanora, we discussed this already." He followed me into the station and stopped in front of the pop machine.

"No, you said, and I disagreed. There was no discussion. But I'm telling you, Niall, as of Monday, I'm back to working a regular schedule. Either that, or you start paying me double time and a half." With that kind of money, I would be tempted to work more, but I knew better. "I have no issues with taking my employment elsewhere."

Niall stepped exceeding close to me. "Is that an ultimatum?"

"Only if you don't hire help. I won't let you work me to

the bone."

"And what about Michael?"

I froze in my tracks. "He'll be just fine regardless of where I work. Him I'll go the extra mile for, but not you, Niall. Not anymore." I filled the three glasses with draft beer and walked past him.

However, Niall wasn't done with me yet. It sucked having a former boyfriend as your boss, even though it had been a long time since we were together. Although he tried, and it probably pained him, he kept the personal stuff out of the restaurant. Better than I was. But not always.

He cornered me and Joy as she danced her way into the station. Seriously that girl leaked happiness out of her with every step. I tried to avoid walking through it. No one should be that happy, all the time. It was weird. That's why her nametag read Joy.

"Joy, can you hold the fort down for a few minutes, I need to speak to Evanora in my office."

"Sure thing," she said, her voice pitching in a child-like voice. "Anything I need to take care of?"

I rolled my eyes. "Nope. I'll drop this off. Otherwise, I'm just waiting on food, but I won't be that long, will I, Niall?"

He gave me a compassionate half-smile which always had the power to defuse my anger, along with a gentle pat on the shoulder. "Not really." He headed to the office at the back of the restaurant, behind the take-out counter, and I dropped off the drinks.

The building Westside occupied was built in the 1970's as an old pizza joint, complete with a take-out area. Aside from the spacious dining area, the rest of the interior was tightly squeezed together, but it was an efficient layout. Our server station was smaller than the average sized apartment kitchen, but held a pop machine, a coffee machine, two taps of draft, a small beer fridge that even held two varieties of cheesecake we offered as dessert, and a small sink. The shelving space around it was packed with supplies.

As I walked through the server station, where I dropped off my tray, I passed the cash register, a definite relic from the 80's, and the take-out area, nestled off to the side of the main entrance. A stainless-steel half wall on my left divided the cash area from the kitchen, where the cooks whipped up the dishes we'd become famous for – our steak bowls. And it smelled delicious.

"What's up?" I folded my arms across my chest. As much as I didn't like being on the floor, I didn't like wasting my time in limbo either.

I stood at the door of the office, or a closet if you really wanted to know. It was like it was designed as an after thought because the office door opened out. Barely room for an office chair, and the built-in desk was big enough for a computer, a few file stands and a cup of coffee with a ring around the inside.

He rifled through a file on the desk and handed me a stack of papers. "Take a look and you tell me if any seem suitable to you." The lone office chair creaked as he leaned back into it, putting his left ankle atop his right knee.

I hopped onto the desk as there wasn't another chair and crossed my legs. My skirt shifted up a little, but whatever. I was no longer his for the taking and he could stare all he wanted. It didn't bother me. "Why are you showing me these?"

"You're the senior server. I figured you'd maybe be able to help me out."

"What does Meghan say?" Meghan was the daytime manager and owner, more surly than me, and not someone I got along with. A huge reason I never worked the day shift.

"She said none will work."

I raised an eyebrow at him and took the file. There wasn't much I enjoyed doing more than proving people wrong.

There were seven applications, and none of them listed serving in their previous experience. Each of them as green as the last hire had been, although I hated to admit it, she worked out okay. Minor spillage and tray dumping, but that was expected. One application caught my eye though and I pulled it free of the stack.

Pushing it into Niall's hands, I said, "He could work."

He read over the application. "He's got no restaurant experience."

"A minor detail. He's trainable and he's willing to work evenings and weekends." I nodded. "A huge plus, since that's where we're short staffed." The daytime shifts were easy to fill, no shortages there. But no one wanted to work late during the week and on the weekends. Except for the romantic duo. Suddenly, I started to miss them being around.

"Fine. Interview him with me," he said as a plea with hope in his voice. Niall put both his feet on the floor and scooted his chair closer.

"Why? I'm no manager."

"Because someday you're going to be."

I laughed in his face. "Not here, I won't."

"Please. I trust your judgement."

"Do you really? That's a first." Even I recoiled as my snarkiness flew out. Well, I didn't mean it like *that*, but it was too late to take it back. Niall's eyes were already wide, the hurt that shone through painfully stabbing what bit of compassion I had left for the guy.

The Adam's Apple bobbed up and down in his throat and he rose, bridging the distance between us, which was already constricting and made me feel like I was being smothered. Way too close for my preference. "You're painfully honest. I think we need the applicants to know what they're getting into."

"So, you want me to drive them away? Because telling them like it is will not work out to Westside's benefit, I can tell you that."

"I need your help."

"Then you're a shittier manager than I expected."

He sighed; a big, heavy sigh. "If we don't hire the right person, Meghan has threatened to become night manager."

Deep down, something in my gut twisted and churned. Her joining the night squad would be a disaster of epic proportions. The limited amount of fun the staff enjoyed now would all be gone. She was a drill sergeant of the highest order. If she switched to nights, I may as well turn in my apron. No way was I going to work under her, and there weren't enough dayside tips to keep it interesting. Niall, I could handle. Her? Nightmare.

I tugged down the hem of my skirt but kept my focus on him. "Fine. Tomorrow night, after the rush. Joy can hold the floor for a few minutes."

"I'll make the call."

"Yes, you will." I jumped off the desk and fanned myself with the heavy, green polo we were forced to wear. "Anything else?"

He grabbed my wrist gently as I headed for the kitchen. "It'll all work out."

Like a bolt of electricity, I yanked my arm back and stared at him smugly. "It'll just take time, right?" As I walked away, I muttered. "You never change." The dining room seemed louder as I approached, but as I scanned it, nothing was out of place. The volume came from a booth at the back where Joy stood loosely, her hand on the back of one of the chairs.

She was chatting up the table of guys, and I pretended I needed a new table setting from the busing station nearest her.

Harmless laughter and good-natured ribbing came from the males, and Joy giggled and grinned the entire time. Joy was a meek and fragile looking lady, so I kept my guard up as a deep instinct to protect those who can't protect themselves roared up inside me. Even though she wasn't my friend, I wasn't above letting her get accosted by men.

I dumped a bus pan full of glasses and plates on the dishwasher rack. Joy followed and dropped off a couple of her own dishes.

"You know those guys?" It wasn't unusual for staff to have friends in, but it's not good to also spend all your time with the one table. If that was the case.

"They're buddies of my brother. We all went to school

together." Unlike my high school years, Joy spoke highly of hers. The prom queen and valedictorian who was head of the student body. How lovely. Gag. Girls like that were typically popular and not too bright. But she graduated five years ago in the top five percent of her class. With smarts and personality and looks like that, why was she waitressing? When I'd asked her, she claimed she enjoyed the variety the waitressing offered and was figuring out what to do for the rest of her life.

Oh-kay. And that was the last conversation we had about post-high school plans.

Joy touched my arm briefly and my eyes fell to the spot as if I'd just been branded. "They're harmless."

"That's good." Still, I'd keep my eye on the situation. It had become second-nature to keep my eyes peeled and my ears open for anything that seemed out of place. I called it motherly intuition, and it usually proved correct.

I balanced my weight on one foot and gave the other a shake, and then switched. My legs ached as I'd been on them since eleven this morning, a start nearly ten hours ago, and I still had two hours remaining on my shift. Twelve-hour days on the weekend were brutal. The money was certainly welcome, but at what cost? Tipping my head to the left shoulder and then the right, I stretched out my neck muscles. Oh man, was I tired.

I bent my head under the overhead counter and asked the cook, "Can I get a side of fries?" I really needed something to munch on. The hangries were raring up.

He passed me a basket of recently cooked fries and I grabbed a shaker of seasoning, coating my dinner in an unhealthy amount of high-blood pressure stimulants. Not that I cared right now. Not much anyway.

Niall walked into the station as I popped a long, heavy-seasoned fry into my mouth. "Finish up your last table, Evanora, and you can go home."

I swallowed. "Sweet."

"You've been here long enough."

"Do I dare ask what caused a change of heart?" I raised my eyebrow at him but didn't wait for an answer.

It was a solid hour before I made it home as my last table camped too long. It never failed—when you want to go home, something prevented it. Exhausted, I parked in the back lot of my house, and stared at the freaking blinds left wide open into the kitchen. I could see clearly inside, and this was not the kind of neighbourhood I wanted to showcase my life to, not even with the roaming police cars that eluded to safety. If I've said it once, I've said it a million times. Once the sun sets, the blinds close. Geezus, it wasn't rocket science. Cracking my neck and shaking out my limbs, I breathed out work and inhaled home. My sanctuary. My peace.

My place was an older style home in a run-down part of the city; a place where sidewalk cracks were the norm, instead of the exception, and cost less to attempt to fill rather than replace. The trees lining the road were old and ancient. Their giant limbs covered the narrow roadway and provided an idyllic look -- if you looked past the weedy, unkempt lawn beside my house, and ignored the dilapidated house facing mine. However, once you stepped onto my front porch and through the door, you'd never know it was in the ghetto.

It came with hardwood flooring throughout the main level, and wall to wall carpet in the basement, which was fine as it took away some of the chill. The walls on the main floor had a light taupe colour brushed across them, and the south facing windows were huge, making the tiny space bright and airy. The bungalow's main floor contained the living room, the kitchen, a full bathroom and two tiny bedrooms barely big enough for a bed and dresser.

But the best part of coming home were the voices I heard as I walked up the back stairs into my kitchen, twisting the blinds closed as I went. Two voices chatted in the living room and I leaned against the wall that separated the back of the fridge from the living room listening for a moment.

"My pick. I've had enough Ninja Warrior," the short brunette said, and pinched the remote out of Michael's hand.

"No, m-m-more." His speech slurred a bit, but nothing I couldn't understand. It would never get better, nor crisper. Sadly, it was also an indictor of the pain he was in. The more the slur, the higher the pain. The more the stutter, the more tired he was.

I silently stood there watching my brother and his aide play and have fun. Such a change from a few months ago when I pulled him out of the hell-hole home he was in. The aides there abused him, mentally and physically, and to a small degree, financially as well. My mother never saw it though and as much as I begged her daily to move him, she never did. When she passed away seven months ago, the best thing about that whole situation was I became Michael's legal guardian.

I got him the hell out of *Billingsgate Manor* and moved him into the empty bedroom in my house. It took a bit of time, but he lightened up and became the boy with the happy smile and positive outlook on life. Something I envied.

"H-hey, look." He pointed in my direction.

"Hey Michael, Melody." I padded around the couch and took the oversized chair in front of them.

"She w-w-won't let me w-w-watch anymore N-N-Ninja W-W-Warrior."

"Because you're tired. It's nearly ten."

"I w-w-wanted you t-t-to t-t-tuck m-m-me in." His hair was dishevelled, the dark brown waves standing out. He reminded me of Flint Lockwood from *Cloudy with a Chance of Meatballs*, but he only had a tenth of the IQ. A ten-year old boy trapped in the body of a twenty-two-year-old man.

"Are your teeth brushed?"

He shook his head.

"Say goodnight to Melody and brush your teeth." I smiled at the goofy grin on his face. "I'll be there in five minutes."

He pushed himself to a stand, taking close to two minutes to do so. I wanted to jump up and help him, not because I was impatient, but for the pinched expression he held. Melody, bless her heart, had told me to only help if he asked for it or truly needed it, or was in any danger. He was in none of those situations, so I sat helplessly and waited. Standing on his own two feet, he walked to the bathroom, slapping his bare feet against the hardwood as he limped his awkward gait across the floor. The door clicked close.

"How was he tonight?" It was a standard question to ask. If anything had arisen, she would've texted me at some point, so nothing major had occurred. Still, as the big sister, and mother figure, I needed to know.

"He was good. A little stiff in the joints, but I think the approaching weather change is the catalyst for that." She was a perky little thing, but oh so good to Michael. From the very first time I met her, I knew she had to be Michael's aide. Kind and compassionate, I never had to worry when she was around.

I removed my Evanora nametag from my shirt and tossed it onto the side table.

Melody laughed as she watched it skitter onto the floor. She bent over and quickly picked it up. "I always find it amusing that they call you Evanora at work."

I countered her laugh with one of my own. "You should see me there, I'm a complete witch. If they're going to give me the name, I may as well live up the reputation."

A few years back, a safety issue arose with the use of our real names on the bills and someone suggested fake names based on personality. When it came to mine, I joked about being a witch but hated the name Glenda as I wasn't pure and good, so some dingbat suggested Evanora, the wicked witch of the east. It stuck.

"I hardly believe you're that bad, Audrina, when you're so sweet with Michael."

"Thanks. I try to keep work and home very separated."

"Oh, you should check out the book." She retrieved a log

book from the table and tossed it in my direction. It had been her idea to give me a rundown of what they did during their time together. I enjoyed the peek into how he spent his evenings while I worked my ass off. Inside was a very detailed running list of the timing and dosage of his medications, and any trips they made into the backyard.

"You took him outside?" I was stunned as I hadn't seen an entry for that in weeks. It caused a smile to bubble up out of me.

"Yeah, it took a while to descend the front stairs, but he wanted out. Wanted to see the woodpecker he heard in the tree up close."

"That's great." But my heart stung a little. I'd tried earlier to encourage some fresh air, but he said no, and I didn't push it. It took way too long to get in and out of the house, and I always worried about him falling and getting hurt. My house was an older house, with tight narrow stairwells and most certainly not adequate for someone with disabilities. It was the main reason I worked myself to the bone, so I could pay for a new deck with ramp. "Should be easier to get in and out soon. The new carpenter's supposed to start around nine tomorrow."

My original guy cancelled late last month, and after I gave him a piece of my mind, he refused to answer my calls. Dammit. I did more research on my number two selection and interviewed Chad, who allegedly should arrive by nine. I rolled my eyes and hedged my bets. Trade workers were never punctual in my experience, yet if you were one day late in paying, they threatened to take you to small claims court. It was ridiculous.

Melody stood and stretched out her petite framed body. Shorter than Michael by a full head, nevertheless she was a powerhouse, her strength hidden under her clothes. Someone better and more qualified than a babysitter. Someone who could help him with any kind of issue. Someone who could love him better on his worst day than our mother ever did on his best. "Alright, I'm going. I'll be back here at four tomorrow?" She ran her hands through her short hair.

"That would be great, thanks."

She walked over to the bathroom and rapped her knuckles against the door. "Night, Mikey."

"N-N-Night, M-M-Mel."

I tucked Michael into bed and rubbed my fingers over his forehead in slow soothing ovals. My knees creaked and groaned from kneeling beside him on the floor, but I wasn't ready to leave. Instead, I watched as sleep overtook my little brother in a matter of minutes. The sweet relaxation wrapped him like a blanket. Confident he was out, I kissed his forehead and ventured the ten steps into my own closet-sized bedroom.

I sat on my bed and opened the white envelope that contained my nightly tip out. It had been a good night, and for a family place like Westside, the tips were decent. Sure, I wasn't making the tips like I could at a fancier place, but I was reasonably content with my earnings.

Hidden in the wall, behind a picture, was my wall safe. Opening it, I added today's cash to the stack nestled deep inside. Things like making a ramp off the front porch didn't come cheap, and the tip money helped greatly. There was no way I was dipping into Michael's government cheques like mother had; those meagre amounts aided in paying for Melody, who he needed while I worked. I preferred cash over credit cards and certainly over cheques. Some people took forever to deposit those and waiting…grr. Besides, in my negotiations, paying cash netted me a small discount. It was win-win for us both. He was paid ASAP and I didn't have a bill hanging over my head. It had taken me a few months of saving every tip dollar, but it was so worth it. Michael was worth it, and he deserved a home that he could function in and out of. Locking the safe, I twisted the dial and closed the picture back over it.

The large 16x20 picture looked right at home; the bright greens and tree bark browns matched my bedding. It was one of my favourite pictures in the whole world, and I adored the story within the frame. We were innocent back then, our youthfulness stretched out before us; I was eight and he was just four. In search of fairies and ghosts, we left the safety of our back yard with our digital camera in hand. We were going to capture one and prove to the world the existence of all things magical. How he giggled as he tromped through chest-high wild grass, hunting and whispering and begging the green fairy to show herself. It was so sweet, I took his picture.

Later when I showed our mother, she claimed the picture as her own, to show off to her friends that she was a good mother, because look, she went fairy hunting in the forest with her children, see? She lied to her friends to make herself look better, but I knew the truth. Despite my begging, she denied me a copy and it was only years later when we moved Michael into Billingsgate Manor that I found the camera card and made myself a giant copy. Housed in a simple Ikea black frame, it reminded me of everything he still was, and how the simple pleasures in life are there if you truly believed.

Dear Reader

I hope you enjoyed the first book of the Ladies of Westside – *Serving Up Innocence* as much as I enjoyed writing it. I really love Shayne and Korey, and am especially happy that they ended up together because in the original draft, they weren't supposed to. She ended up with someone else, and someday I'll post the alternate ending. Watch www.hmshander.blogspot.com for the extra content and sneak peeks of the next three books in the series (and find out about what happened to Lily). Now that you've read about the characters, whose story are you most interested in reading? Evanora's? Joy's? Meghan's?

As an author, it makes my day when someone shares their thoughts and gives me feedback on the characters you've invested your time with. It's thanks to the early beta readers that the rest of the stories came to be since they wanted to know more about Evanora and Joy, and even Meghan, figuring because she's such a raging bitch, her story could be quite saucy. Share with me what you liked, what you loved, or even what you hated. I'd love to hear from you.

Contact me via email (hmshander@gmail.com) or via my website (hmshander.com).

Finally, I need to ask you a favour. If you are so inclined, I'd love a review or a rating of *Serving Up Innocence*. It doesn't have to be long, even something as simple as "Loved it, looking forward to the next one" works. Reviews and ratings help me gain visibility and as I'm sure you can tell from my books, reviews are tough to come by. As a reader, you have the power to make or break a book. If you have the time, please post a review on Amazon or Goodreads.

Thank you so much for spending time with me.

Yours,

H.M. Shander

Other Books by H.M. Shander

The Charlotte Cooper Set

Run Away Charlotte
Ask Me Again

The Aurora MacIntyre Trilogy

Duly Noted – book 1
That Summer – book 2
If You Say Yes – book 3

The Ladies of Westside Series

Serving Up Innocence
Serving Up Devotion
Serving Up Secrecy
Serving Up Hope

Acknowledgements

Gosh, it's hard to believe I am writing my sixth public thank you. Sixth! I'm in a perpetual state of shock. A million thanks to my family – Hubs, The Teen and Little Dude – and to my parents. Where would I be without your support and endless cheerleading? Thank you for giving me time to sit and write while you played your games, so I could make my daily word count. Thanks for all your help with signings (especially you my little PA – you are always out there smiling beside me and helping people pick out their swag.) Love you always.

To my tribe of critique partners and alpha readers and beta readers. Lacey, Emma, Jeannine, Julie, Mandy, and Dylan. Thank you from the bottom of my heart for all your comments, advice, wisdom, and pointing out what didn't make sense and what needed to be expanded on. Thank you for falling in love with Jasper and Jade and seeing them through to the end.

To my cover designer Cassy – Great job! I had a blurred vision when I hired you to design all four covers for the series, and although there was some struggling with nailing down that first cover, after some searching, I think it's perfect. I'm so thrilled we worked on this together, and I look forward to adding many more covers designed by you.

To my editors at Infinite Phoenix and IDIM Editorial– You had your work cut out for you. I know the story wasn't the high drama and conflict you're used to, but I appreciate your comments and suggestions to make the story better. It was a huge struggle for me to change so many things, but it worked out for the better. I hope.

If I missed you, it certainly wasn't intentional. I know I couldn't be where I am without the help of so many others. Thank you! And thank you for reading and making it all the way to the end. You all rock.

About the Author

H.M. Shander knows four languages—English, French, Sarcasm and ASL—and speaks two of them exceptionally well. Any guesses which two? She lives in the most beautiful city in Canada–Edmonton, AB; a big city with a small-town feel, where all her family live within a twenty-minute drive, although her parents are contemplating moving away. As much as she'd love the beach under a blanket of stars, this is her home.

A big-time coffee addict, she prefers to start her day with a hearty mug of java (her favourite being a double double from McD's) before attending to anything pressing, but sometimes it must wait as she shuttles her kids off to school via the #momtaxi. No complaints though as she knows the children soon won't rely on her and instead, she'll be left to listen to the many character voices in her head, telling her what they're planning next. She's a self-proclaimed nerd (and friends/family will back this up), reveling in all things science, however likes to be creative when there's time. Right brain, left brain? Both.

Did you know she once wanted to be a "Happy Clown" as she enjoys making people smile, but she's beyond terrified of scary clowns? How ever many different jobs she's worked, her favourite has been working as a birth doula and librarian, in addition to being a romance author. Because, let's be honest, who doesn't love falling in love?

Five things she loves, in no particular order; The Colour Blue, The Smell of Coconut & Shea Butter, Star Wars (the original three), The Ocean, and Chocolate.

You can follow her on Facebook, Twitter and Goodreads. She also has a blog (hmshander.blogspot.ca) she writes on from time to time, and posts extra *bonus*chapters from published stories.

Thanks for reading– all the way to the very end.

91781428R00136

Made in the USA
San Bernardino, CA
25 October 2018